KEEPER OF SECRETS

STEVEN M. SCHORR

AGNI HUNA
PUBLISHING
SAN ANSELMO, CA

Keeper of Secrets

Steven M. Schorr

1998
Agni Huna Publications
San Anselmo, California 94979 USA

Copyright © 1998 by Steven M. Schorr

All rights reserved. No part of this book may be reproduced or transmitted in any form or by any means, electronic or mechanical, including photocopying, recording, or by any information storage and retrieval system, without permission in writing from the publisher except in the case of brief quotations embodied in critical articles and reviews.

Cover art: Steven M. Schorr, Steve Fischer
Cover design: Steve Fischer
Book design and layout: Steve Fischer

ISBN 0-9663587-0-8
Library of Congress Catalog Card No. 98-96137

Published by:
Agni Huna Publishing
P.O. Box 51
San Anselmo, California 94979
www.agnihuna.com
rajagni@pacbell.net

First Printing 1998

Printed in the United States of America

Dedicated to my loving family,
for their patience, perseverance and courage.
Especially for Lynn.

Table of Contents

The Landing	1
A Meeting	13
A Test	25
Crumbling Temple	37
The Moon and Venus	55
Step Pyramid	69
The Guide	93
The Night Watchman	105
Origins	111
The 'Cairo'	123
The Sacred Mission	135
The Vision	149
Of Ka, Ba and Aakhu	157
A Teaching Preserved	173
The Hand of Fate	181
Epilogue	195
Glossary	199

Chapter 1

THE LANDING

    The wheels of Flight 614 touched down on the baked tarmac with the grace and sizzle of butter hitting an overheated frying pan, bouncing and belching black smoke with each impact, as the jumbo jet kissed the earth and rolled to a stop. Enthusiastic applause erupted from the otherwise docile passengers who graciously praised *Allah*, Jesus or any other attending savior. A good landing in the land of the pharaohs is any one where the plane remains in one piece, and not splayed into a million shards of steel over the Mediterranean.

    Richard Allen Jansen, known by close friends and acquaintances as "Raj," strained hard to see the debarkation ramp as he gazed out the port window through ripples of heat rising off the runway. There was none close by; in fact, there wasn't a building in walking range. Flights originating outside Egypt and landing at Cairo International Airport were routinely taken to the far end of the runway where passengers deplaned into waiting buses. This discouraged the wanton detonation of explosive devices that would otherwise ruin a perfectly good airplane. Raj understood the safety factor, and was glad to be on the ground in one piece.

    The air hit Raj as he emerged from the plane like the first blast of steam in an American Indian sweat lodge. It was unexpectedly thick and hot blowing in from the desert and convecting off the asphalt runway. Wearily stepping down the mobile staircase toward a waiting bus he noticed heavily armed soldiers strategically positioned around the plane. Each carried a cocked standard-issue Egyptian Army M-16, should any "unexpected" event occur. They were positioned in a defensive perimeter displaying fearless arrogance as they directed the passengers to "move quickly, move

Keeper of Secrets

quickly."

What a welcome, he thought, adjusting the shoulder straps of the weighty gear bags. He pushed back his long black hair and adjusted the dark wire framed sunglasses that had slid down his nose. He opened the top buttons of his shirt and checked his multi-pocketed vest, making sure his passport and other essentials were accounted for.

One by one the passengers began boarding the extra-wide-body bus until it was crammed with sweaty, dazed passengers with their carry-on bags. The air within was stifling and the heat soon became unbearable. One more overloaded passenger was crammed in, and the bus doors hydraulically slammed shut. Sweat poured generously from Raj's forehead. He could feel his shirt pasted against his skin. The weight of his bags cut hard into his shoulders and made him wish he'd traveled lighter, though the time for that decision had long since passed.

The bus paused while men with walkie-talkies engaged in unintelligible banter. Raj waited for the bus to begin moving, thinking of a cool glass of sweet Egyptian tea. The thought was of little comfort. With a sharp jerk the bus began to move. Raj caught his footing and peered out to the empty tarmac. Tired passengers clung to the hand straps like sides of hung beef, leaning in unison with each bump and curve. Their expressions revealed their bewilderment as they moved toward the aged terminal whose sign cheerfully proclaimed "Welcome to Cairo".

They were ushered up a stilled escalator, frozen in place like the petrified remnant of a vanished technological age. Each passenger struggled to enter the terminal, hurrying at first but then forced to wait in line. There they were scrutinized by the presiding commandant whose function was to find suspicious looking passengers. Each groan of disapproval was met with calculated indifference as the line filtered through the "welcoming" gauntlet.

Raj inched forward in line, breathed a sigh of relief and started through the gate without incident. Why all the fuss? he wondered. By his third step a stern voice called from behind.

"Wait, wait. I must see your passport."

Raj paused, hoping the voice was directed at someone else. Two soldiers appeared in his path, rifles drawn across their chests. He caught the eye of a soldier to his left who unblinkingly grimaced as he flexed his firearm in a threatening motion. Raj flinched and turned to break eye contact.

"You, American," barked the Commandant, pushing past the crowd toward Raj. "Passport, I must see your passport." His thick Egyptian accent produced a distinct roll on the 'r' of passport.

Raj hesitated, but realized it was not the time to open up a discussion. "Here," he said, as he handed over the small, worn, blue book.

Raj had traveled extensively over the years, from Amsterdam to Tahiti, with stops in Istanbul, Oman, Peru and Israel. His passport would have been the envy of most world travelers and was so full of visa and entry/exit stamps that an addendum of accordion pleated passport paper had to be stapled on. He knew that travel to some countries was a "red flag," and worried that although he couldn't possibly be a target for their investigation, he might be today's scapegoat.

"Has anyone tried to contact you?" began the interrogation. "Are you carrying any packages or documents from anyone whom you do not know? Has anyone approached you or talked to you in a suspicious way? Where are you coming from? Why are you here? Has anyone you do not know asked to meet with you? Do you know about the holy war, the Jihad?" All these questions came at Raj with rapid-fire directness leaving little time for response. He tried to answer where he could, but mostly only shook his head shrugging quizzically to each query.

"You must come with us," was the final pronouncement.

Raj was in shock; after all, what had he done? And why was he being singled out from the crowd? He began to follow the

KEEPER OF SECRETS

Commandant, his eyes fixed on the floor. They were interrupted by a commotion at the back of the line. An argument ignited between two passengers who were soon shouting at each other. Raj understood nothing, but noticed the Commandant's attention shift to this new event. He seemed alarmed and handed Raj back his passport as he went to investigate. Without the slightest acknowledgment, Raj was set free. He breathed a sigh of relief and continued to the main baggage area.

    Many years had passed since Raj last visited Egypt. He thought back to his first arrival, noticing how little had changed: same frenzy and urgency, similar faces, all unknown and filled with mystery. A journey to this fabled land was always filled with mystery, he thought. His mind raced as he looked around the interior of the terminal. It was crowded beyond comfort with passengers from dozens of connecting flights. Around him the Arabian cultural dress code made for a pageant of robes, tunics, kadifayahs, turbans, veils, *niqab*, togas and assorted headdresses of all forms and colors. Each revealed its country of origin and ethnic family traditions. As the luggage began to roll off the carousel, mountains of packages, boxes, trunks and suitcases tumbled in geometric chaos, with everyone scrambling to pull off their personal belongings. Boxes were marked with multicolored twine and bold faced lettering in both English and Arabic. It was difficult to break through the jam of passengers to retrieve his bag, but the crowd relented with a few shoves. Retrieving his gear, Raj made his way to the next check point.

    Eyes followed him as he made his way through the crowded corridors of the terminal. Eyes of seedy-looking men with dark ruddy complexions, cigarettes ever present, faces veiled by thick puffs of smoke. Eyes from behind the niqab, female eyes barely visible, dark and lined with Egyptian *kohl*. Eyes of policemen with machine guns slung at the ready. Eyes of porters who raced to grab baggage which might then disappear. He was a stranger in a land born of a different God, a man whose culture and experience could not know of this ancient desert womb, or of the cloth that wrapped the Arabic mind.

"Passports. Have your passports ready," was the announcement that squawked on the loud speaker, punctuated by static noise as a steady stream of travelers funneled into lines at the immigration terminal. People pushed and shoved as long lines formed, some for foreign nationals, some for locals. Again, hurry up and wait.

"Mr. Jansen, Mr. Jansen," called a handsomely dressed woman. "Mr. Jansen, Mr. Jansen," she repeated.

"Over here," Raj replied.

She quickly made her way over to him looking a bit surprised, perhaps by his youth or general appearance.

"I am Tamera, and I have been sent by the Giza International Hotel to escort our guests." She grabbed firmly onto Raj's arm. "We can assist you and bring you through customs. We also have a car waiting outside to take you to the hotel. Please, give me your passport."

"Uh sure, OK," he said. "Thanks for coming to meet me."

"Your welcome," Tamera continued, "this is a special service to our guests, because we know how difficult this part of the journey can be." Her accent was unmistakably Arabic, but her speech revealed a certain refinement and a familiarity with western expressions.

Raj was surprised but delighted. Anything to speed up the bureaucratic hassle was welcome.

"Please, you must exchange some U.S. dollars for Egyptian pounds. I'll need $140 U.S. dollars."

"What?" Raj exclaimed.

"Yes, please," Tamera said. "This is a Government rule."

"Sounds like the price of admission to me. Well, 'render unto Caesar'..." Raj knew this was coming and feigned surprise. It is a regular practice for some countries to force their guests to relinquish hard currency on the way in. The quest for good foreign exchange is the life blood of many countries.

After making the dollar exchange and getting his passport stamped, Raj was cleared through immigration. With the help of Tamera, who clearly knew the ropes and the key officials, he passed to the front of the queue and was on his way out of the airport. The long walk to the vehicle area was lined with the relatives and friends of other travelers, each looking expectantly as he passed like a runway model showing off the new spring line. He knew no faces, and heard no one calling his name. He just walked on as the cries of the awaiting crowd echoed around him, like a prodigal son returning home.

As they entered a black Mercedes Benz sedan, Raj realized he was the only guest being picked-up that day, and that he'd be riding with Tamera alone. This is rare in a culture that keeps its women covered from head to toe. He was also glad to see that she was dressed in western clothing without the niqab.

The niqab is a traditional Arabian garment designed to partially or wholly cover the female face and sometimes the entire body, except for the eyes, which peer out mysteriously from "behind the veil." In the West, this garment might be seen as an imposition to a woman's right to express herself, but in the Muslim world it's quite normal and considered customary attire. Unlike other Arab nations, however, Egyptian culture allows for both the traditional Islamic dress and the modern style adopted by many who are influenced by the West.

Tamera spoke with an air of culture and poise. She appeared to be in her late twenties, and had a soft voice with a slight but distinct accent, one that was softened from travel and international study. Working for a hotel chain required a university degree and fluency in several languages.

Her long brown hair fell down her back in soft ringlets. Her light, coffee-colored complexion was offset by large hazel eyes, thickly lined with kohl. She wore cherry red lipstick and light blue eye shadow and had on a thin gold necklace and gold post earrings.

THE LANDING

She wore a black skirt and suit jacket over a white blouse which adequately covered her, even though it was quite warm. Women who embrace a western style must still display modesty when in public in the Islamic world. She leaned carefully toward Raj, having unbuttoned the top of her blouse. Tamera was demure but projected an exotic sensuality that was undiminished by her businesslike attire.

He was entranced by her gaze. Her eyes locked on his and her proximity brought the smell of jasmine perfume to his senses. Breathing deeply, he filled his lungs tasting the jasmine deep in the back of his throat.

Where have I seen her before? he thought. She looks so familiar. What is it about her? Why do I feel like I know her? The depth of her stare, perhaps. She touched him in a way he rarely encountered.

"So, what brings you to Cairo?" she asked.

"I'm here on business," he replied, breaking eye contact to look at an obelisk stationed in the median of a passing intersection. He was always amazed when he saw these neglected ancient monuments in their modern settings, like so many abandoned props from an old Hollywood movie.

"Really, and what might that be?"

"I trade in antiquities and artifacts," he said, "but mostly I just...seek."

"Well, if you are looking for antiquities, you've come to the right place. We have plenty of those. We've been making them for thousands of years. In fact, it's a major industry here." She explained how many families lived in towns settled next to the funerary monuments where they made their living from the tombs. In some cases, they played roles in the discovery and exploration of some of the most famous tombs, like that of the boy Pharaoh, Tutankhamun. From an archeologist's point of view these scavengers are considered a nuisance and a destructive force on the tombs and artifacts. Their plundering of grave sites left many tombs in shambles, especially in the Valley of the Kings at the Necropolis of Thebes. There, grave robbing has developed into an art form, with many looters making their fortune probing the burial grounds. The robbers are a problem for the Egyptologists, but the people are just poor and are only filling a need. "Visitors have been coming here for millennia, and they always want to take a piece of Egypt home with them. They have even perfected the technique of making new things look old. You must know that even some of these 'new artifacts' may be hundreds of years old. But really, I'm curious, just what are you seeking?"

"Experience, maybe wisdom," Raj replied, coyly.

"Wisdom? Is that all?"

"Wisdom and the way of the ancients," He replied, deliberately remaining vague. Raj had studied the world's ancient cultures, a study made meaningful by the profit realized by trading in valuable artifacts. Although self-taught, he had audited courses at some of the world's most prestigious universities, studying with the leading authorities in the field. His interest in archeology was furthered by the considerable time he spent at the antiquity collections of such great museums as the Metropolitan Museum of Art in New York and the British Museum in London. That, along with time spent traveling to historic sites, gave him experience and an innate sense of the history and value of various relics. He made it a personal quest not only to gather rare artifacts, but also to understand the cultures that produced them.

They both fell silent as their car approached the Nile. The river's expanse broadened their view, from the crumbling old buildings that lined the streets and avenues of Cairo, to a broad swath of silvery gray water lined with palm trees and studded with obelisks and other monuments. Raj could see the passage of fellucas sailing gently up and down the river, sails billowing in the afternoon breeze. The boats' movements appeared as random meanderings of color and form–an impressionist's scintillating dream.

The Nile, river of Gods, is a nurturing presence woven into the lives of countless millions. It is essential, not only for those who make their life on the narrow ribbon of green that straddles her banks, but also for those whose remembrance of her is buried deep in their subconscious, so deep that it reaches back, before birth, to a repository of memories containing past-life experiences. Countless waves of human incarnations have lived on her shores, some in servitude and others as rulers of the great pharaonic dynasties. Many have also found the Nile in dreams, in visions of a place that was once the cradle of humankind's ascent into civilization. Perhaps all are drawn back to her shores to complete their cycles of learning and experience.

The Nile is also an expression of the Great Mother, for all life nearby is sustained by her waters. Were this land to be without this grace, a parched and barren choking dust would blow upon an empty valley, as is the case for the land which rises beyond the fecund sash which clings to her shores. It is because of this fertile land that the Nile attracted its early settlers, those who sought her sustenance and made their homes in her embrace seeking succor from the inhospitable elements beyond her protective reach. Certainly, any pre-historic explorer seeking a home would have made one by her banks, and set down roots to grow a civilization. One thing was abundantly clear as Raj looked southward up the river at the immense city that straddled her banks–the settlers never left.

They crossed over the Zamalek bridge and headed out Pyramid Road toward the Giza plateau. With the Nile behind them, Tamera raised her luminous eyes framed in light by a reflection from the afternoon sun. She inhaled deeply and asked Raj, "How long are you planning on staying with us?"

"That all depends on what I find," Raj said, the spell of the Nile experience now giving way to fresh input from the sights and sounds of the aged Cairo streets speeding by.

"Perhaps I can assist you," she suggested.

Keeper of Secrets

He thought about her statement for a moment. He could have shrugged off her advance and politely declined, but how many opportunities are derailed by fear or suspicion? How many critical opportunities are passed by in favor of safe and well known paths? Can a life be changed if one surrenders to the destiny of the moment, especially when guided by the heart? To that he knew the answer.

"Yes, please," he responded with a sigh that released all resistance.

"I think I should introduce you to my cousin Omar. Perhaps he can help you find what you're looking for." Her tone became pensive as she glanced out the window. "He's a man who has seen and done much, and he knows Cairo very well. When we get to the hotel I'll call him."

Raj's was excited by her suggestion, knowing that a good contact was exactly what he was looking for. The best opportunities particularly in a place rich in history and its artifacts are always through someone knowledgeable in the ways of the land. If her cousin Omar were such a person Raj knew he'd find what he was seeking. He only needed to trust his inner guidance, and be led to the source.

As they drove up Pyramid Road the Great Pyramids loomed more distinctly with each passing mile. At first, the triangular shadows on the horizon seemed vague, almost as if they were an apparition with uncertain solidity. But as they drew near, their unmistakable presence commanded and finally dominated the view. Raj was in awe. Nothing can compare to being in the presence of the largest man-made structures on earth. They inspire the kind of respect and reverence that few objects in the world can.

"I see you have been smitten by our wonderful pyramids," Tamera said, noticing his amazement.

"Yes, they really leave me speechless."

"Then you're lucky to be staying at our hotel. No other can boast the view that we can. I'll make sure that you have a room in the old part of the hotel. It has an unobstructed view directly across from Cheops."

"Thank you, I appreciate that," He replied.

They pulled up to the entrance of the hotel where a doorman in an elaborate uniform, festooned by a traditional fez, opened the car doors and greeted Raj warmly.

Tamera got out and, arranging for his bags to be picked up by the bell hop, turned to Raj saying, "I'll leave you here to check in. Perhaps you'll want to rest or freshen up after your long journey. I'll call you as soon as I reach my cousin. Bye now, nice to have met you."

He watched intently as she walked away but, tired from the long flight, all he could do was think about a hot shower and a comfortable bed.

Keeper of Secrets

Chapter 2

A Meeting

The phone rang pulling Raj out of an especially lucid dream. In it he saw himself as a bearded, turbaned aristocrat, resplendent in the purple robes of royalty, on a visit to a Central Asian scent shop. There he was sampling exotic incense, each scent wafting up in a dancing veil of smoke as its substance flashed on a bed of red-hot coals.

It was the shrill bell of an old phone that tore Raj out of his dream. He couldn't recall where he was, but the phone kept ringing. Finally he reached over and answered, fumbling at the hand-set.

"Hello, hello," he said, still groggy from the wrenching transition.

There was no answer.

"Hello, hello, anybody there?"

Still no answer.

"Amazing," he said, as he dropped the hand-set back onto its stand.

He yawned and closed his eyes, his thoughts now drifting back into a fuzzy state where dream awareness meets conscious wakefulness. As he recalled his dream he was drawn back into its field of play into the realms between dreaming and consciousness, known in esoteric schools of thought as the "Diamond of Consciousness." Perhaps he could receive a message, or connect with his dream and understand its meaning. Where had he been? What did it mean? It felt as though he was visiting another time and place, maybe even another lifetime. He reached for his watch to see what time it was. How long have I been asleep? he thought, as he checked his watch. "Four-thirty a.m., God, I must have been tired," he mumbled. He lay motionless for a while before deciding to get up. The meaning of his dream was out of reach, with the memory fading fast as thoughts about the day ahead began to crowd in. Although he had a sense of having experienced a past life, the mechanism of the wrenching phone call from "no one" seemed like a gift from the beyond, awakening him at that precise moment, to bring him into a state of remembrance. Had he been contacted from within his dream, he mused, or was he awakened from his dream to recognize the experience of a past life? He really didn't know, but the experience was certainly unusual. It felt like a subtle touch from the beyond.

As the dawn's first glow appeared Raj drew the curtains back from the hotel window. He stared in amazement at the sight before him. *Cheops*, the Great Pyramid, was unobstructed and no more than a thousand meters away. Where else in the world can you wake up to this? he thought.

Raj enjoyed taking time in the morning to stay in shape. He needed to stretch his six foot frame and tone up his lean muscular body, which he did with a combination of calisthenics and yoga postures. At 35, he thought it was important to keep in shape.

After a brief workout and a hot shower, Raj ordered a continental breakfast from room service: croissants, hot coffee with cream and sugar, yogurt, and some fruit, devouring it soon after it arrived. Then he settled back for a few moments of meditation, to gather his thoughts and center his energy. *Sadhana*, his spiritual work, brought him a profound sense of peace and provided a renewed clarity which he drew on during the day. He never felt right unless he did this work, feeling that it connected him to divine guidance providing protection and grace.

As he finished his morning ritual the phone rang. He reached over from his half lotus posture, left leg crossed and folded over his right, and answered "Yes."

"Hello, Raj?" It was Tamera.

"Tamera, *Sabah al-khair*," Raj said, pronouncing a thick glot-

A Meeting

tal 'kh' sound as he spoke, greeting Tamera with the Arabic equivalent of "good morning".

"Oh, *Sabah al-nur*, Raj. I see you've learned some of our language, how sweet." Tamera's tone was especially light and happy. "I hope you are up and ready for an exciting day. Have you had your breakfast?"

"Yes," he replied. "I already ate, and I'm looking forward to whatever the day may bring, *Insh'Allah*."

"Ah, Insh'Allah," she responded, surprised by his familiarity with the phrase.

Insh'Allah is an all-purpose Arabic exclamation, with a deep religious tone, literally translated as "by the Grace of Allah," or "by the Will of God." It is also used in other applications ranging from "we'll see" to "let it be done".

"I've arranged for you to meet my cousin Omar. He said he would be happy to meet you and share his insights. Omar is an intuitive man who is in-touch with his feelings. He is like a school, and has many students here in Cairo. He seemed to be open to the idea of your visit, and must have sensed something positive about you. Perhaps he can help you find what you seek. I'll have a car come and pick you up at ten a.m. Please be in front of the hotel. I'll meet you there."

"I'm looking forward to meeting your cousin, but I'd really like to spend time with you," Raj answered.

"I'm sure that can be arranged, Insh'Allah," Tamera said coyly. She knew in her heart something had been awakened sensing a special attraction that was beyond the physical. It was from a deeper level of being–a sensation of the heart.

"See you at ten, *ma salama*," he said, as he softly hung up the phone.

Ma salama is a familiar form of good-bye, the Arabic equivalent of "go in peace". He enjoyed saying simple words from the local dialect, and did so wherever he went. He usually got a lot of mileage out of a few well chosen words. He would learn their exact

Keeper of Secrets

pronunciation and articulate them flawlessly, peppering his conversations with them. This would always delight the locals and provided a bridge for communication. In fact, there were a number of occasions where his perfect pronunciation would launch an extensive one-sided conversation, leaving him in the awkward position of having to explain that he didn't understand a word of what was being said. If he was lucky an English-speaking friend would come to his rescue. If not, he would just nod or smile amicably. Sometimes a single well placed word from the local dialect could make the difference between success and failure. Although Raj could only speak English he found this strategy worked well. The locals would always be pleased that he showed enough interest to at least try learning their language. But occasionally it worked against him, and he would find himself a party to conversations carried out in front of him where the other participants knew he didn't understand a word of what was being said.

He gathered up his day trip essentials: sunglasses, passport, cash (in Egyptian pounds), camera, extra film and his notebook and pen, put them in his shoulder bag and left the room.

He reached the hotel lobby at 9:45 a.m. with enough time to look around. It was ornately decorated in the fashion of an old Victorian ballroom with gilded colonnades, hand-carved crown molding, and red velvet walls. This was the old part of the hotel which still had a style suggestive of a time when its splendor was reserved for visiting kings and dignitaries. The place exuded an atmosphere of regal presence.

Raj wandered over to the lobby newsstand to get a newspaper and catch up on world events. The front page of the International Herald Tribune, contained the troubling headline: "Jihad Terrorists Explode Bomb In London". He read it intently as he walked to the front door to await Tamera and his ride. It was upsetting to see the destruction and death caused by extremist organizations, especially now that he was so close to them. Their fanat-

A Meeting

ic followers had no face and little regard for life or property. They were unconcerned that the people whose lives they destroyed had plans for the future, or children to care for. Their goals were often obscure, but their rhetoric was usually aimed at the establishment of a non-secular Islamic state, the destruction of Israel, or hatred towards America. Raj knew the Jihad fighters were active in Egypt, and he hoped to avoid contact with them.

Tamera appeared at a little before ten, smiling cheerfully. She was dressed casually in a fine, loose fitting white cotton blouse with a flowing ankle length flowered skirt. She radiated a charm that seemed to light up her surroundings. Raj walked over to her and gently touched her shoulder. She turned and smiled.

"Sabah al-khair, Raj. I see you have been waiting. I hope not too long."

"Oh no, I just arrived," he said, as he positioned himself so that the sun was out of his eyes. "You look beautiful today, Tamera. Thank you for meeting me. I hope I'm not interfering with your schedule." Raj didn't know if she was accompanying him or not.

"Oh, its quite all right. I have some time-off due me so I've elected to take the day and go with you. Besides, its been ages since I've seen my cousin Omar. He's so much fun." Turning to see if the car was coming she continued, "I'm very excited about today, I have a feeling that we're in for an adventure."

"I hope so," he replied.

The car pulled up to the hotel driveway at exactly ten a.m. It was a 1965 Rambler in mint condition and still exhibiting its original white and turquoise color. "So this is where they keep all the older model cars that disappear from the streets of New York," he said, chuckling to himself. She didn't get it. Owning an automobile was still a luxury in Cairo and not possible for most people.

They both got into the back seat of the car and nestled into the worn, white leather seats. Tamera spoke to the driver giving him directions to an address somewhere on the Nile island of Zamalek, and the old Rambler sped off trailing a plume of gray exhaust.

"I trust you slept well. Have you recovered from your jet lag?" Tamera's concern seemed genuine.

"Yeah, I was out as soon as I hit the bed." That was almost true, as he had lay down to rest with Tamera still on his mind. "But I was awakened by a strange phone call at 4:30 am. I picked up the phone, but no one was there."

"Probably a wrong number. It sometimes happens on our outdated telephone system. The hotel operator must patch in the calls by hand. Perhaps it was a slip of the hand."

Raj admired Tamera and was especially aware of her scent. He had a heightened sense of attraction as she pressed softly against him in the tight confines of the Rambler's back seat.

Crossing onto Zamalek, the car stopped in front of a cream-colored building, one of many that lined the streets of a fashionable neighborhood. Tall Acacia trees, ten to twenty meters high, lined the sidewalks providing a welcome shade. The driver let them off and Tamera led the way through a side alley down a long corridor and into an interior courtyard surrounded by the inner walls of a six-story apartment building. Through a private entrance they came to a large wooden door and rang the bell. Soon a tall man with gray hair and a pencil-thin mustache appeared.

"Tamera, my dear, how wonderful to see you. *Ahlan wa sahlan*, so good to see you." They hugged briefly and exchanged kisses on both of their cheeks.

"Ahlan wa sahlan, Omar," Tamera replied.

"This must be your American friend. Mr. Jansen, I presume? Welcome, welcome to my humble home. Please come in. Can I get you something to drink?" He immediately clapped his hands and called out some instructions. "How good of you to come and visit me. I am so glad you have met my lovely cousin. It is not often that I get to see her these days."

"Omar, you flatter me. Thank you for inviting us on such short notice," she said.

"Yes, Sabah al-nur," Raj added. "Thank you for opening up

A Meeting

your home to me. Please call me Raj. I've only been here one day and I already feel at home in your beautiful country."

Omar led them into the hallway and said, "Please come in, so we can take refreshments and talk. I want to hear of your travels. I am sure that we will have much to discuss." He continued in thickly accented English, "In fact, I've had Zina prepare a suitable place in the outdoor garden where the shade will make our visit most comfortable. But first let me show you my home."

They entered a large room with an arched entryway and a high vaulted ceiling. The room was so large it dwarfed its contents, including three ornately carved dark oak cabinets with beveled glass doors. Each contained what appeared to be numerous examples of early Pharaonic ceramic sculpture. These immediately caught Raj's eye, but they continued walking. The floor was covered with a fine hand-woven Turkoman rug, the kind with eight hundred knots to the square inch, upon which sat a heavily carved coffee table inlaid with a marquetry scene of the Abu Simbu monument. On two walls were large tapestries depicting caravans of camels crossing the desert, with men in turbans and women draped in flowing garments. On a third wall were several framed discolored photos of Omar's parents, grandparents and great grandparents. It was dark in the room, despite it being late morning, as light entered through other adjoining rooms whose windows were covered in layers of intricately stitched, lace curtains. The main room adjoined a spacious foyer which led to the dinning room and kitchen. Off to one side a long corridor connected five or six other rooms. It was a large apartment that seemed to have been built in the early nineteen thirties. The place had a refined quality about it, having been well maintained.

After the brief tour, Omar led them out into the garden courtyard which, despite being located in the middle of an apartment building, was peaceful and secluded. It was filled with tropical plants: areca palms, fig trees, broad leaf philodendrons and young banana trees, all cultivated in giant earthen pots. Privacy screens made of a split-reed material were hung strategically around the courtyard creating the illusion of a separated enclosure. Toward the center was a white canvas tent-like structure suspended from several ropes. The top of the tent was partially open with three sides completely enclosed while the fourth side remained open and drawn back by thick braided red ropes. Within were several overlapping oriental rugs of different origins and sizes upon which were placed an assortment of overstuffed satin pillows, three rattan chairs, and several hand-painted leather ottomans. This made for an exotic retreat, drawing on the style of the desert people that settled Cairo. Incongruous to this "planned exotica" were the laundry lines that hung from the windows of the apartments above. They were full of multi-colored undergarments, fluttering like Tibetan prayer flags on a Himalayan monastery *stupa*.

Omar motioned to Raj and Tamera inviting them to sit on a chair of their choice, while he assumed the central position on a large winged-back, wicker chair. The chair created an aura-like effect framing Omar's commanding presence. As they settled in, Omar's maid Zina brought out a large *Sheesha* water pipe and some related supplies. She filled the lower section with fresh water and fired up a small charcoal brazier before getting up to leave. Omar said something to her and she nodded obediently disappearing into the main house.

Omar chatted in Arabic with Tamera with an occasional English word thrown in for emphasis. Raj could understand none of it, nor was he threatened by their need for privacy. He was happy to sit quietly in the splendid surroundings, listening to the sound of their conversation.

Soon, Zina reappeared carrying a large serving tray. On it was a crystal decanter with a long thin neck, along with three clear glasses set in silver holding frames, plates, utensils, and a large filigreed dish filled with an assortment of baklava-type pastries drenched in honey and covered with pistachio nut crumbs.

Zina passed out the glass cups and plates and placed the pastries on a table located in the center of the tent. She went around to each of them, starting with Tamera, and poured a stream of steaming hot mint tea from the decanter. This was done in the traditional Egyptian tea-serving style, where the pitcher is held high above the glass and the tea is poured in a long, steady stream. Having accomplished this in good form, Zina received a thankful Arabic cheer from Tamera and Omar. It was an impressive show that brought smiles of delight. Raj found the tea to extremely sweet, but very satisfying despite the heat of the day. As the pastries made their rounds, he loaded his plate with four pastries, each better than the last. He was an aficionado of this Middle Eastern delicacy.

Omar turned to Raj, his demeanor becoming serious. He leaned over and remarked quietly, "You have come to visit me, and you are an honored guest in my home. I know, from Tamera, something of your quest here in Egypt. You must know that the Government has outlawed the taking of any kind of antiquities. Their paranoia knows no limits, and enters into every aspect of our lives–into what we say, what we read, what we think, and what we do. The Government is a powerful force, not to be taken lightly."

Raj nodded in agreement and mumbled, "I understand."

Omar continued with great urgency, "The lines have been drawn and the battle has been declared between the forces of free expression and those of state repression. And now, this unfortunate circumstance is being inflamed by the rising power of the fundamentalist *Jihad*. Both wish to stem the tide of free thought. Both wish to impose their control on the free exchange of commerce and ideas. Both use the struggle against each other, a struggle for the hearts and minds of the people, to intensify the fighting, pitting friend against friend, brother against brother. This battle for power effects everyone, and no one is untouched."

Raj was a little shaken by Omar's intensity, but appreciated his candor. He felt like he was being thrust into a hotbed of local politics and was uncertain how to react or where Omar was going with the thought.

"We, however, are a resourceful people and everything has its price." He took a sip of his tea and continued, "Before I can do business with you, you must pass a test. You see, I've had some problems with Westerners and their appetites. They do not always measure up to their presumed...," Omar paused, then thoughtfully completed his sentence, "capabilities."

Now Raj was beginning to see the picture. This was a moment of scrutiny, and his future relationship with this man was in the balance. He peered at Omar and said, "I'm not sure which 'Westerners' you've been hanging out with, but I'll hold my own in any situation you can offer. What do you have in mind?"

"Here in Egypt, we smoke the sheesha, not just as a pastime, but as a ritual–a way of life. For this ritual, we prepare a special mixture of natural herbal ingredients. When smoked they release their power into the mind of the participant. We mix *habow* from the cannabis plant with local grown tobacco and a special sacred plant, *Salvia divinorum*. We prepare this carefully and fire it with hot coals. This we inhale deeply through the sheesha. The water of the sheesha will cool the smoke, but its power will seep into every cell of your body, your mind, and your thoughts. Here, we consider the Sheesha Ritual to be a sacred act. A bond of brotherhood is created by those who engage in this act for, under the influence of the ritual, one's inner thoughts are revealed. If you are strong of mind and heart, the sheesha will test your mettle. Then, if you desire, you can enter into my world where anything can be accomplished. We follow the 'laws of God', not the 'laws of men'. If you wish to do business with me you must cross over to the world where heart and mind are joined. We live in a dangerous world at a dangerous time, and I must know your heart's intention unobstructed by any false facades and stripped of any of pretense that may conceal deceit. This we can only do by crossing over to the inner realms–on the wings of the smoke."

Raj took Omar's words very seriously. He was no stranger to

A Meeting

smoking or otherwise consuming the sacred plants that are used to alter consciousness. That custom, documented in the chronicles of all cultures since the dawn of history, has long been supported by seekers of knowledge and understanding. Raj grew up in the sixties and seventies and was a participant in the consciousness expanding revolution that created a global counter-culture. He had tasted the forbidden fruits that unlocked the "doors of perception" and encountered the inner planes that were accessible only to those who passed through that door. Raj had trained to use these mind-altering substances as a prelude to the more austere disciplines that could lead him further on the path of expanded awareness. Knowing full well the risks that were involved, he understood the state of mind necessary to circumvent the law and take command of his own consciousness–a right, he judged, natural and God-given. The laws of men set limits on consciousness and put road blocks in the path of self-exploration. These laws deny the opportunity to experience the true relationship between awareness and the vast, unbounded universe of perception. He rejected the rules that try to rein in thinkers who step beyond the boundaries of accepted convention seeking to explore the evolution of human thought . And so he had no problem with the request of his host and eagerly consented to the test.

"Omar," Raj said, "you have opened up your home to me, and I am honored by your hospitality. You have revealed your world to me, inviting me to participate in your sacred ritual. I am deeply moved that you have seen, in the short time that we have known each other, that I am worthy to 'cross over' with you, to the inner realm, so that I may join you in brotherhood. I accept your invitation. I am ready for the test."

"Ah, *kways,* very good," Omar said, genuinely pleased. "Tamera," he said, turning his gaze toward her, "you were right, this is a good man, a man of conscience and respect, one who is ready to take the next step."

Tamera turned to Raj and said, "Are you sure you want to go

ahead with this Raj?" She seemed concerned.

Touched he replied, "Tamera, I live for these moments."

Chapter 3

A Test

Zina worked the charcoal brazier and with nimble movements of her wrist fanned the coals to an iridescent orange-red glow. With each wave of her cardboard fan, the coals flashed in a display of heat and light. Tamera prepared a mixture to fill the removable pipe bowls. There were twelve baked clay bowls laid out on a small prayer rug, in three rows of four. She began by kneading a large piece of reddish-brown habow in her palms, intermittently heating it over the burning coals until soft. The tobacco and Salvia plant were prepared by cutting the leaf material into small workable pieces. Next, the habow was heated until it began to crumble into fine granules and was mixed with the plant material. The mixture, called *Mota*, was worked until it was evenly blended and skillfully packed into each bowl.

Omar assembled the sheesha and tested the fittings to make sure it had an even draw. Raj could hear the bubbling of the sheesha as Omar sucked on the intake hose, forcing air through the water of the pipe. This bubbling action helped to filter and cool the smoke.

Omar, seeing that all was ready, began to speak. "My friends, thank you for being here. This is a sacred moment, one destined to be, and consecrated by Allah, *Il'humd'Allah*, that we may gather as friends to join our hearts and minds in the name of truth, Insh'Allah. Let only truth be shared here, and may we know that truth in trust and love. *Bis'm Allah Al Rahman el-Rahkim*" These words, spoken in reverence, are words of power for the followers of Islam, always regarded with respect and veneration.

Having finished the benediction Omar started to sing a soft Arabic dirge. He closed his eyes and rocked back and forth in a slow deliberate motion inducing a trance-like state. Everyone joined in, singing or humming along with the melody, each adding harmony to Omar's steady dirge. Their voices merged in random resonant tones as their passions ebbed and flowed. The chant continued until it reached a crescendo, when Omar suddenly stopped and fell into a deep meditative silence. Raj could feel a calm, solemn devotion present. Silence prevailed until the sounds of the outer world began to filter in. Omar breathed a long sigh, opened his eyes and said, "It is time to begin, Insh'Allah."

With that pronouncement, Zina placed one of the clay bowls onto the pipe, carefully adjusting the bowl to make sure it was securely fastened. She handed Omar a long thin hose with a wooden mouthpiece. He took the mouthpiece and ran his hand along the connecting hose to smooth out the kinks in the multi-colored, thread-covered tube. It untwisted like a snake awakened from a deep slumber. Placing the mouthpiece gently to his lips, he signaled to Tamera. She moved over to the charcoal brazier and, grabbing a set of charred metal tongs, reached deep into the burning mass of coals to find a perfect-sized ember at the peak of its scorching intensity. The coal was placed carefully in the clay bowl on top of the mottled green mixture. Omar began to suck vigorously and inhale on the sheesha hose with a staccato like action that caused the Mota to ignite with ferocity. Each in-breath brought the fire from the coal deeper into the Mota. Each in-breath brought the piercing smoke deep into his lungs, drawing its substance into his blood stream and then to his brain. With each inhalation he arched his neck backward as he deliberately held the smoke in his lungs. With four puffs, Omar was saturated with the Mota, which swirled and undulated around his head like the ocean fog rolling over the Golden Gate bridge into San Francisco Bay. Through that thick translucent cloud he passed the mouthpiece to Raj, who took the hose with evident anticipation.

Raj said nothing as he accepted the hose of the sheesha and placed the worn wooden end into his mouth. Glancing at Tamera, who sat fully absorbed tending the coals, he inhaled the Mota slowly and cautiously. After the Mota turned to ash, Tamera carefully removed the bowl and replaced it with a fresh one into which she placed another hot coal. Raj proceeded to draw the smoke deep into his lungs. He could feel the movement of his chest and the streaming of smoke through his mouth and throat. With each inhalation, a stimulating warmth crept up his spine to the back of his head. A rush of energy pulsed through his arms and into his hands, with a tingly sensation felt at his finger tips. He was experiencing an increased sensitivity to sound, and a distinct change in his visual acuity.

Raj paused, inhaled again, and passed the hose to Tamera. He watched as she smoked the sheesha in a delicate, refined fashion. Reaching for his tea cup, he drank the warm liquid, clearing the acrid taste from his mouth.

"Ah," Raj exclaimed, breaking the silence. He turned toward Omar, and with a broad smile affirmed, "*Shukran, shukran.* Thank you my kind host. I feel the Mota within me and my heart opens to its gentle caress."

"You are most welcome, my honored guest. It is a pleasure to share our sacred ritual with you, that you may experience the true, living soul of Egypt."

The sheesha passed back to Omar. He sucked on the mouthpiece with renewed vigor, like a baby nursing on its mother's engorged breast. He seemed to draw strength and succor from the sheesha's issue. With a precise cadence the clay bowls were cycled and recycled, as each bowl was emptied and refilled. The sheesha went round and round, and with each pass they renewed their commitment to the ritual. Omar exclaimed "Il'humd'Allah," after each completed bowl. Raj did likewise. Zina poured more tea, which served as the lubricant between fiery puffs, until the pace of smoking slowed. Omar put down the mouthpiece as shafts of sunlight pierced through the dissapating smoke penetrating to the courtyard floor. They were very relaxed and in a state of deep introspection, each in their own world.

"Do you feel the energies emanating from all living things?" Omar asked.

"Yes, I think I do! I can feel them," replied Raj. The synapses of his brain were flooded with receptor-enhancing chemicals from the Mota, resulting in an expanded awareness.

Recognizing that Raj had entered an altered state, Omar opened up, sharing his train of thought. "We human beings are symphonies of resonant energy, pulsating in vibrational interdependence. We can see this as we penetrate the 'veil of awakening' and perceive the worlds within."

Raj felt transported down internal pathways of insight. He closed his eyes to experience his imagination effected by a spontaneous explosion of activity within his brain. He heard Omar's words and allowed them to transport him to new realms of insight.

Sipping his tea, Omar took a deep breathe and continued. "All matter is really energy. Our bodies are composed of this energy. We exist where the substance of the material world issues forth. This is the flesh of God; our so-called matter.

"Because of the brain's gross perception we see, feel and sense life's apparent solidity. Yet, we come to understand that the particles which comprise matter are separated by enormous distances. Actual physical substance occupies very little space. Matter as we see it is mostly 'not there.' It is energy in space held together by a mysterious force. This is the 'life force.' Without the life force matter cannot exist, and will break down into uncoordinated energies. The life force propels evolution by inducing resonant harmony, which effects every atom of our being.

"Our life depends on this force, because it supports and sustains us. So powerful is the essence of life that we cannot exist without it, yet we are unconscious of its presence. We must come to recognize and approach this essence, for it is the key to unlocking the mystery of being. But we must realize that it will not reveal itself to us until we are ready, and only when we approach with solemnity.

"To know our essence we must first come to know our soul, for only our soul is subtle enough to touch the essence of being. To understand this is our most sacred duty."

"Omar, your wisdom and insight touch me," Raj offered. "Your discourse has evoked a deep sense of understanding, for me. It is always exciting to share the perceptions that come from one's beliefs, especially those expressing a delicate web of knowledge. I see you have spent some time exploring the inner realms."

"Yes, it is my duty not only to open the doors of perception, but also to facilitate the journey as well. When we have crossed the 'veil of awakening' we have a sacred responsibility to receive subtle impressions from that realm and retrieve those gems of wisdom to share with others. The world is in great need of the true wisdom born of direct experience. We can find this in the vast inner reaches of the unexplored human consciousness."

Omar pensively stroked his mustache and with concern, looked up at Tamera and said, "Tamera, my dear, you have been so quiet. How are you?"

"Oh *kwayiesah*, thank you, cousin. I am speechless with wonder just trying to follow your words and their meaning. Raj has grasped the meaning; he is a seasoned explorer of these realms. You both seem to be on the same wave length."

"Yes, we are," said Omar.

"So, Omar," Raj said, feeling the effect of the Mota diminishing in his consciousness. "I am ready for the test. What is it?"

"Oh!" Omar exclaimed, laughing at the notion. "The test! Well, you already passed."

"Already passed, really?" Raj was both relieved and surprised.

"Yes, you see, the test was a way to see if you could take the Mota. Let me explain. Some six months ago, I was entertaining an American guest. We were sailing the Nile at night under the moonlight in an old felluca. The felluca owner is a friend of mine. I always rent his boat, as he gives me a special price for an evening's sail. So, we loaded the boat with food and drink and the sheesha, and spent the night on the river. It was a beautiful night, full of stars, the constellation Orion clearly visible in the night sky. The breezes were quite refreshing, a welcome relief from the heat of the day. We were sailing for some hours and began enjoying the sheesha when, after some time, my American friend fainted. I suspect that, with all the wine we were drinking, it became too much for him. Anyway, his stamina was depleted and he was unconscious. I became alarmed so I decided to head for shore to bring our comatose friend back to his hotel. We pulled into the dock at about one a.m. to a place close to where my car was parked. The dock was at water level, and a long ramp traversed up the high retaining wall connecting the dock with the street above. As my friend was quite heavy, I decided to carry him myself. I lifted him up and draped him across my shoulder with his head dangling over my back. I carefully made my way out of the boat and began walking up the ramp leading to the street. When I got about half way up the ramp, a high-powered flashlight cast its beacon on me from above and a voice called out, 'Halt, halt, what are you doing there?' It was a policeman, and he wasn't happy at what he was seeing. Can you imagine my having to explain the American draped over me, unconscious, like a sack of beans?" he said, laughing.

"Well, somehow I talked my way out of that situation, but I swore after that I would be more discriminating about the guests I entertained, and I would make sure of their ability to endure our kind of mind-altering activities before extending any invitations to our private rituals.

"So, I had to test you, and now I know, my friend, that we can work together." Omar was ebullient at the outcome of the 'test' and got up from his seat. Turning to Raj, he said "Please come with me, there is something I wish to show you."

Raj followed him out of the courtyard through the maze of plants to his apartment. They entered and walked through the foyer down the long connecting corridor. Omar turned left at the end of the corridor and walked into a large office lined with enclosed glass cabinets. He sat behind the desk and pointed to a side chair, inviting Raj to be seated. Reaching over to an electric panel located behind him, he turned on one of several switches. The cabinets lit-up with a warm glow, to reveal a treasure trove of Egyptian artifacts.

Raj was amazed at the sight and exclaimed, "Omar, this collection is incredible!"

Raj had spent a great deal of time exploring the Cairo Museum, which contains the finest collection of Egyptian artifacts ever assembled in the world. Not even the Metropolitan Museum of Art in New York, whose collection is substantial, could compare with the depth of the Cairo collection. Of course, as in any museum collection, what was on view to the public was only a small percentage of their total accumulations. He could only speculate on the incredible finds that jammed the basements of museums. At the Cairo Museum, the artifacts represented the entire chronology of Egyptian history, and contained objects such as rows of massive stone statues and the small household deities called *Ushabtis* that accompanied the deceased to the afterworld.

"You must know that the demand for Egyptian artifacts has been very strong lately," Omar said. "I have been rather fortunate to be in the right place at the right time. I have many associates who have been bringing their finds to me for years. Some of these artifacts are good and some are not, but I always buy whatever they bring me, no questions asked. And, I always pay a fair price. Of course, I suspect that many of their finds were looted from the tombs that dot the Nile Valley. Actually, most of the tombs were looted long ago by our grandfathers and great grandfathers.

"Occasionally someone uncovers a special tomb, one which was so well hidden that only erosion or some accident led to its discovery. When this happens, my associates will have their pick of the artifacts before the authorities can arrive, or shortly thereafter. My finders are very loyal to me. Our families have lived here for hundreds of years, as far back as anyone can remember, and we have always been in the antiquities trade. But wait, there is more to see."

Omar opened a hidden panel to his right and pulled an obscured lever. An innocuous-looking cabinet containing some interesting stone statues of Horus and Isis began to move, pivoting on a central fulcrum. It slowly turned to reveal another glass-covered cabinet. Within was a heart-stopping sight. The cabinet contained a collection of museum quality objects including gold jewelry and statuettes rivaling the most precious pharaonic artifacts he'd ever seen. The best piece among them was the funerary mask of a young pharaonic heir. The craftsmanship was of the highest order, from the Middle Kingdom era. The features of the mask were carved in gold and inlaid with gems and precious stones. The eyes were made of ivory with black jet pupils, and it was adorned with necklaces of amethyst, carnelian, lapis lazuli and turquoise beads.

"This is incredible," exclaimed Raj. "I didn't know such collections were in the hands of private individuals."

"This and much more," Omar responded. "While it is true the Government has confiscated most of what it can find, and of course the newer finds are all government controlled, many of the artifacts surfacing now have been carefully hidden and guarded by local families for generations. They are passed down from mother to daughter, as an insurance against hard times. We knew these valuable heirlooms were around, but now with difficult times for many families (they grow so large and what with dowries for the girls), we see many rare objects surfacing..." He trailed off lost in thought, then continued, "The objects you see before you are a small part of the available treasures now in private hands. The biggest problem is finding suitable buyers for these artifacts and getting them out of the country. There are very strict rules which prohibit the exportation of antiquities, especially those identified as important to our historical heritage, and they have all been so considered. The authorities will spare no expense to prevent them from leaving

A Test

the country.

"The government is watching very closely to see where these pieces turn up. If they are found they will be confiscated. The dealer will be severely punished with heavy fines, and usually his entire collection will be impounded. It has become a dangerous business." Omar's demeanor become more solemn as he let Raj digest all that had been revealed.

Raj was excited by what he had seen, thinking he'd found the "mother load" of available Egyptian artifacts. He wondered about the prices of these treasures, but had a general idea of what they might be worth. Silently, he calculated the middle man profits for some of the artifacts in the specialized collector markets that trade in rare antiquities. He stared at the gold-filled cabinets realizing that a friendship with Omar could also lead to a valuable opportunity. He began thinking about the logistics necessary to bring the artifacts out of the country. These thoughts had an intoxicating effect on Raj's state of mind.

Suddenly, an explosive pop echoed off the nearby courtyard walls, sending a chilling jolt that broke the golden spell. "What was that?" Raj exclaimed with urgency.

Omar's face turned pale. The shock he expressed was genuine and unstudied. He flew back in his chair at the sound, though he used the momentum to his best advantage by flipping the switches to the moveable cabinets. The cabinets began to slide and turn to their secure, lock-down positions. This hid the most precious artifacts by replacing them with other, less valuable, pieces.

They heard footsteps moving swiftly down the hall. Tamera came running into the house in panicked desperation. "Omar, Omar," she cried, screaming something in Arabic. "Quick, we must get out of here, now! You are being 'visited' by some of your 'friends' from the Jihad," she said sarcastically. "They came into the courtyard looking for you, very agitated. Two men, one small, one large, both bearded, with black leather coats and dark sunglasses. They said you know why they are here, and that they are here to see you, personally. The smaller one pulled out a silver pistol from under his jacket and fired it in the air. These are madmen. Omar, we are in serious danger."

Omar grabbed his coat as he leapt from his chair and ran for the door. "Follow me out the back door," he yelled.

Tamera and Raj were right behind, as Omar ran out of his office and into another of the rooms. He ran straight to a closet and, swinging open the door with one hand, reached in with his arm to spread open the coats that blocked a spring loaded, false-backed door. They all bolted through the door with Omar closing up behind them.

"Those bastards," Omar said, as he stopped to catch his breath, "I just paid them last week." He was more mad than shocked, as they continued to run out the rear of the building. "We'll take my Jeep. I park it several blocks away as a precaution."

Omar proceeded to explain, "The Jihad enlists many of us in the 'business' community to assist them financially. At first, this is mostly done in an innocent way, by donations to a good, local, religious group. They use our money to help their schools and orphan programs. This is the least a good Muslim can do! But, they find out from the friends they make in the community who in the neighborhood has money and why. Soon, we are visited by their soldiers, those militant ones who carry out the orders. We don't know who they are, they are not our friends. They just come with the power of the gun and demand their tax, their tribute. Against this kind of extortion we can do nothing. We cannot go to the police for fear of retribution, nor do we wish to be discovered by government agents for our antiquities trading. The Jihad operatives will stop at nothing to get what they want. I am a lover of life, a free trader. What to do? What to do?"

They were heading out to the street when they heard a second shot in the distance. They started running faster and gained some ground, but their armed assailants were still in pursuit. Omar realized that this was probably just a scare tactic, and that no one would be hurt, but he couldn't be certain. Normally his contacts in the Jihad were more reliable and could protect him from the more unstable, radical elements of the organization. He also knew that some of these extremists could snap, without provocation, and act irrationally. This was, however, a matter that could be handled in a diplomatic fashion–later. He knew the right palms to grease, and how much grease they required. For now, he thought it best to leave as quickly as possible to protect Tamera and Raj.

By the time they reached the white canvas-top jeep, they could see their black-coated assailants turning the corner about two blocks away. They quickly got in the Jeep, with Tamera in the back and Raj riding next to Omar. Within moments they pulled out of the parking spot.

Omar was reasonably sure they hadn't been seen, but proceeded with all due speed. He drove to the main intersection, a large round-about traffic circle, veering hard right and fighting to control his vehicle's momentum. Entering into traffic he took another right at Pyramid Road–the road to Giza. He drove about a mile before realizing he'd lost the gunmen back on Zamalek. They were silent while their adrenaline levels dissipated and their heart rates returned to normal.

"We cannot go back to Zamalek." Omar said, "That would be too dangerous. It would be much better for us to go out to my farm at Abusir and wait there. I have a safe house at the desert's edge down the hill from the ruins of Abusir. I'm sure you will find it an interesting place. There is food and drink there, and we will be well taken care of. Later, I can go back and straighten this out."

They were happy that Omar had a plan, because the terror of the moment was very unsettling. Both Tamera and Raj were pale and winded from the chase and were glad to leave it behind.

Tamera responded in a weary voice, "Yes, I agree this is necessary. We should stay away from Zamalek, but how can we be certain that we will be safe at Abusir? Do you know if the Jihad can find you there?"

"Perhaps," suggested Omar. "But I think these thugs are just taking advantage of the absence of my good friend, Dr. Wahid. He made all the arrangements for my protection and I trust his judgment. The good doctor has a firm grip on his militia friends and they are usually well behaved. These men who attacked us are from the outside. They could not know of the Abusir farm. I'm sure we will be safe there; besides, there are easier targets than me, elsewhere in Cairo."

Raj agreed to go with them to the farm. Not that he had a choice. He felt there was a reason for this turn of events and wanted to know what it was. "I'm all for the farm. I'd like to see Abusir," he said, matter-of-factly.

Omar turned left and began to weave down neighborhood streets lined with disintegrating mud brick shacks, an occasional camel, and hundreds of young children playing by the sides of the roads. He made his way south following the green edge of the Nile Valley's western limits. The congested city streets gave way to verdant fields of crops, populated by water buffalo and farmers tending their fields. Small villages filled with simple mud huts conical in design and primitive in construction dotted the fields. This basic structure has served for millennia, built and rebuilt with each passing season of floods that washed through the valley. Now, the Aswan dam has changed that; the regular flooding cycles come no more, but the housing styles remain as they have for millennia.

They rolled through the countryside slowly slipping back in time as city life gave way to the time-honored traditions of rural existence. Raj was happy to get outside of metropolitan Cairo and experience the countryside, especially after a being chased by angry gunmen. He was mostly happy to have escaped from a 'too close' encounter with the Jihad.

Chapter 4

CRUMBLING TEMPLE

Omar's Jeep rolled up a narrow dirt road lined on either side by stalks of corn in full maturity. He honked the horn several times to inform the caretaker of his arrival as they pulled up to a cluster of small white buildings at the end of a long driveway. An old man ran up to Omar and kissed his hand. They conversed in Arabic and exchanged greetings. Omar instructed him to make a fire, grill some corn, and prepare flat bread and other foods for his guests. They got out of the Jeep and stretched, walking about somewhat disoriented by their ordeal. Though it was late in the afternoon, the sun felt hot against their skin.

"Welcome to my country home," Omar said in a relieved voice, assuring their safety. "Please relax, take your time and look around. I love this place and should probably spend more time here. Every time I return I'm very happy, and every time I leave I'm very sad. What to do? What to do?"

The land was almost flat, comprising about twenty hectares, well irrigated, and surrounded by rows of tall, lush, date palms. To the east were other farms slightly below Omar's following the course of the river. The verdant Nile Valley stretched north and south as far as the eye could see. To the west of the property arose a large bluff crowned by a crumbling hill. On closer inspection, Raj could make out a series of tall colonnades on the side of the hill. The hill was littered with large, broken walls and assorted stone debris–clearly an ancient ruin. Giant stones which were slightly visible beneath the desert sands marked a path leading from the direction of the Nile. Raj was astounded that an entire ruin lay just up the hill from Omar's farm. It was as if he had his own private archeological site to explore.

Keeper of Secrets

"Come with me and I'll show you around," Omar said. First, he brought them over to the irrigation well to show-off his precious water supply. An eight-inch pipe protruded from a large, mud-brick, pump house. He had Abdul, the caretaker, turn on the large diesel engine that ran the pump. Within a few seconds, an abundant stream of fresh, clear water poured vigorously into the irrigation canals that fed the fields of corn and rows of sweet date palms. He also showed them a vegetable garden full of a variety of melons, tomatoes, peppers, onions and eggplants, as well as a small herd of goats and some chickens. The farm was, for the most part, self-sufficient.

Abdul and his family were poor tenant farmers and grew as much as they could to sustain their basic needs. Of course, the major share of all that was grown on the farm belonged to Omar, but he was more than generous in making sure that Abdul and his family were well taken care of.

They walked over to the main house, following Omar as he entered. The house was a modest structure constructed with white-washed mud-brick walls, and a mud and straw roof that rose in a tall, conical shape from the squared walls of the main house. The interior of this peculiar roof gave the appearance of a planetarium dome, as if the arc of the heavens had opened up within. Large window openings fitted with wooden shutters gave the house a light, airy feeling. The floors were made of wood, and were covered with palm-frond mats. The house had several rooms including a kitchen, and one bedroom with a large antique brass bed covered with a white feathered comforter. Omar used the house as a retreat to escape the noise and pollution of the city. He kept few possessions there, preferring to live as simply as possible.

Abdul and his family lived in a small hut adjacent to the main house in an enclosed compound that also included a goat pen and a small tool shed. He was an unpretentious man, lucky to serve a man like Omar who treated him well. Abdul appeared to be in his late sixties, with deeply grooved, leathery skin. He had the kind of skin that comes from a hard life working the land, constantly under the hot sun. His laugh revealed a gentle happiness, with few teeth evident in his smile. He lived with his young wife, who never came out of the hut, and seven children who scampered around the grounds. The children were shy but curious at the arrival of new guests. Abdul spoke no English but had a good sense of humor, so laughter was their means of communication.

Abdul prepared a small feast of hot corn on the cob, fresh goat milk feta cheese, hummus mashed from chick peas and garlic, baba ganooj made from puréed eggplant, and sliced red tomatoes from the garden. In a small wood burning oven he prepared pita bread whose aroma beckoned them to helping after helping. They talked and laughed about the day's events, but mostly ate while Raj and Tamera listened to Omar converse with Abdul. Abdul brought out a plate of newly ripened dates, which everyone quickly ate. They washed it all down with thick Egyptian coffee made in the traditional style, extremely sweet with a layer of ground coffee-bean mud on the bottom of the cup.

"This is really wonderful," Raj said, the coffee giving him a nice buzz. "I can't remember when food has tasted this good."

Omar concurred. "This is a special spot, filled with the blessings of the Nile and the *ka* of the pharaon who walked these fields thousands of years ago. Their energy can still be felt, especially around the temples and sacred sites." He paused and said, "Tamera, why don't you take our friend Raj up to the Temple of Abusir? It is one of many important archeological sites that follow the Nile Valley south, toward Luxor and Aswan. I think Raj will be quite impressed to have a private showing. I will stay here, as there are some things I must take care of. You know the way. Be careful when you climb on the stones, as they can become dislodged. This can be dangerous and can also harm the temple. I'll see you when you return. Insh' Allah."

Raj and Tamera walked slowly from the house across the fields toward the temple. At the far end of the field the Sahara abruptly began. The boundary is clearly marked by the stark contrast between the lush green living land and the sterile, lifeless sands that stretch west to the Atlantic. There is no in-between here, the desert either owns the land or it doesn't. Almost always, the Sahara is the dominant force in the geography of Egypt, but where water can be found or brought to the desert's edge, life can be established and the land reclaimed. It requires a great deal of perseverance to undertake such a battle. Without resistance, the desert will soon undo generations of hard work in a single wind storm, blowing its dunes in an unrepentant mass across everything, including the most well planted fields. The natural power of the wind and sand can be overwhelming to even the most persistent human measures.

They crossed the "line of life" and entered into the empty desert lands. No locals lived on or owned this land. The Government made sure of that by establishing an archeological park surrounding the temple, a buffer against human encroachment. Rarely would the locals venture there.

They followed the path where the stone causeway emerged from the sands. They walked alone. No throngs of tourists, no tour buses, no parking lots, no souvenir shops, no locals...no one.

Strewn along the path were millions of broken pottery shards, some brown and some gray-black. The sands were filled with small stones and crumbling debris caused by time's slow, elemental decay. Even mountains must wear down, and these stone monuments were on their way to becoming dust.

The Pyramid of Abusir dominated the landscape with its asymmetrical eroded sides. Abusir is an example of pyramid structures built in the lower Nile Valley after the Great Pyramids were completed five thousand years ago. Somehow, the craftsmanship and engineering knowledge used in the construction of the Great Pyramids of Khufu, Chephren and Menkaure, were mysteriously lost. The Abusir pyramid had suffered extensive erosion and loss of its stone surface with the integrity of the outer sides almost completely gone. It was difficult to differentiate between the pyramid and a simple eroded hill. The Temple of Abusir, however, was a different story. Though stripped of its once formidable grandeur, the foundation stones and standing walls revealed an extensive temple complex.

Raj could feel a certain sense of remembrance wash over him as he walked toward the temple grounds. Each step took him deeper into the energies that emanated from the compound's vicinity. It was as if he had been there before. The thought sent a shiver down his spine and brought up goose bumps on his skin. He felt a special sensation, which he knew as a spirit presence. His heart opened in resonance, a feeling that he trusted as the confirmation of truth. He knew he was close to something extraordinary.

"Do you feel as though you know this place?" Raj said, turning to Tamera.

"Yes," she answered, entranced, "but not because I've physically been here before. I have the strangest feeling that I've walked this causeway in the distant past. It's a familiarity not born of recent memory, but of a direct knowing from beyond. My knowledge of this place is not from this life; I believe I was here in another time as another person."

"I'm having the same experience." Raj concured. "I think it's a *déjà vu* triggered by the power of the place. The events that have occurred here have charged it with a distinct energy. This place has been magnetized, perhaps from ritual worship performed here over the eons by the high priests of some ancient order, or perhaps by the buildings themselves. The energy here is so strong that I feel it rushing through me." He stopped for a moment and shivered. "Whoa, I just felt another surge of energy going up my spine. It's coursing through my body. I feel vibrant and alive. I feel activated. Tamera, I think we were drawn here to experience something. I need to know what and why."

"Well then," she suggested, "let's continue to explore the temple grounds. If there is something we must experience, it will become apparent soon."

They continued, entering a wide concourse made of perfectly fitted monolithic stones. On either side were the crumbling foundations of boundary walls. This led in an uninterrupted pathway to a large compound and into a main hall. Under foot were perfectly level mammoth floor stones. Colonnades supporting ornately carved buttresses stood beside precisely matched stones made of polished granite. Large sections of the walls were etched with representations of ancient Egyptian deities. As they proceeded further into the far reaches of the main hall, other side rooms came into view. They turned and entered a side room whose walls were covered with detailed hieroglyphic writings. They stopped to examine them, noticing that little was still intact, having been faded and bleached by the relentless scorching sun.

"Tamera, do you know what any of this means?"

"No, Raj. I can speak and understand four languages, but not ancient Egyptian hieroglyphic. It's a specialty reserved for professors of archeology at the universities. Anyway, very few of the experts really know what was being said or what the language actually sounded like. These are the lost memories of our ancestors. We can only hope that we understand a little of the true meaning of the writings."

"Think of the possibilities of contacting those ancient thoughts." Raj offered. "What a richness of insight they could reveal. By looking deeply into the past, we could bring those thoughts back and make them live within us. Think of the understanding that could be realized from a direct experience of those times and events. This could be possible if we were to enter into a trance vision. Once there, we could share the memory of a past-life experience, explore the events of that time, and somehow penetrate into the essence of those moments. We could experience their thoughts and feelings, bring their tongue to life and animate their expressions. Perhaps, we could even repay a debt or fulfill a karmic obligation. We might be able to carry on a deep emotional longing, or consummate a hidden, suppressed love, one that may have waited thousands of years for the right moment, to bring the right souls into perfect alignment."

"Raj, look at this," Tamera suggested. She had found a long square tunnel hewn into the massive stones, forming a break in an otherwise solid wall.

"Amazing!" Raj exclaimed. "What skill or technology could have created a perfect square tunnel carved into solid stone?" Now it was apparent that the temple had different levels which could be accessed by this passageway. With no hesitation, he made his way into the tunnel. "Follow me in, and we'll see what's on the other side. I suspect this special tunnel led to the secret initiation chamber of an ancient religious school, or perhaps to the burial chamber of a noted priest or dignitary." The tunnel sloped down at an angle of about thirty degrees and ran a length of twelve meters, where it emptied into another room on a lower level of the complex.

They crawled down the shaft, crouching down slightly to fit, but still remaining on their feet. Emerging at the other end of the tunnel, they found themselves in a large room surrounded on all sides by steep, smooth vertical walls about ten meters high. The walls were open at the top, revealing the azure blue cloudless sky. Before them was a monolithic stone sarcophagus whose lid was carved from a single piece of gray granite. It was three meters long, two meters wide and one meter high, and must have weighed several tons. It had been wedged open at the seam and had a visible gap between the top and bottom, where looters removed its precious contents centuries ago.

Raj went over to the sarcophagus lid and ran his hand over the smooth granite, still warm from the sun's rays. There was a slight patina of dust, as fine as talc, which made the surface of the stone extra sleek. He marveled at the craftsmanship required to quarry and dress such a large piece of rock, thinking of the man-hours it must have required. Taking off his T-shirt he cast it aside, and laid down on the sarcophagus lid with his arms crossed as if mummified. "Tamera," he called out, "take a picture of me lying here for the record."

She took out the camera and took a picture of him. "Raj," she said, as she finished shooting, "wait there a moment, I'm coming over."

Raj lay there looking up at the sky, trying to sense what it must have been like to have been buried in a tomb. How the soul of the deceased must have hovered above the mummified remains of the dead body, as the ceremonial attendants lowered the gilded casket into the giant stone sarcophagus. He shivered at the thought of those poor souls who were buried alive, sentenced to die a horrible death in servitude to their masters. Putting his hands out by his sides he felt the slight arch that formed the main section of the sarcophagus lid. The radiant heat of the stone was comforting to his naked back, as the sarcophagus and the entire funerary chamber were now in the shade of the late afternoon.

Tamera climbed up onto the lid and stood at one end, by Raj's feet. She looked down at him in a sweet and endearing way. Raj marveled at her beauty, her dark, henna-accented hair unbound and flowing past her shoulders. Her curvaceous body was visible, silhouetted through her sheer skirt and framed by the temple walls.

He was intensely attracted to her and motioned for her to come closer. She walked up to him and stood directly above him straddling his waist, her long skirt glancing his legs and billowing slightly in an errant breeze. Tamera stretched, and in a subtle way she signaled her acquiescence to his unspoken desires. He motioned for her to sit, and she slowly lowered her knees to the granite lid. He could feel the warmth and pressure of her body as she positioned herself. He slowly reached under her skirt and felt her soft skin and the powerful muscles of her legs. Carefully, he ran his hands up her thighs, stroking and massaging each inch. She moaned lightly at his touch. His hands moved to her inner thighs. She grabbed her blouse and with both hands, in a single movement, pulled it over her head and flung it off. Reaching behind her, she unclasped her bra. He raised his arms and gratefully filled his hands to overflowing. She sighed and reached down to undo his belt and jeans, the final barrier between them.

They embraced and began their dance, moving together in a slow rhythm. Each pulse of their bodies became synchronized. She lay down on him and they turned, still locked in an embrace, carefully maintaining the cadence of their movements.

They continued to make passionate love, every inch of their skin sensitized as they touched. With each movement, waves of memory washed over them. Taking breath for breath, their chests rose and fell together in an instinctive, sympathetic rhythm. With each movement they penetrated more deeply into the other's being, beyond the body, into the soul. They sat up and, still locked in an embrace, began to stare into each other's eyes. Soon their surroundings seemed to vanish as their attention became more inclusive.

Raj concentrated on Tamera's essence. He began to swim in the unfathomable depths of her gaze. Slowly, he saw her face begin to change. It was dissolving and transforming from that of Tamera to a face less familiar, yet one he was certain he'd known somewhere before.

Her features were smaller and her skin darker. Her eyes became almond-shaped and were accented with dark black eyeliner. Her eye color changed to deep brown with wide black pupils, while her hair became black and straight. In her hair were woven golden threads adorned with beads of silver and lapis lazuli. He also detected a subtle change in her scent, which became infused with the essence of jasmine mixed with patchouli.

"Tamera," he said in amazement, "as I look at you, you seem to be another person!" He asked himself, could this be a hallucination? Or was he experiencing a genuine perception of the soul's awareness manifesting as an ancient past-life memory?

He started to explain his vision and how he was creating it, so that she could share in the moment with him.

"I've relaxed my gaze as I look at your face, so that my eyes are slightly out of focus. Then, I look beyond the focal point, beyond the field of light that we generally see as solid reality. This shift of the focal point allows me to see a subtle energy, where I can observe a transformation occurring. The more I see of this image, the more I realize I know this person. Memories cascading into my mind detail the events of her life and my relationship to her. These memories are my own! Yet, I have not lived them in this life. These memories are real to me, as real as any I've ever had. They speak to my heart, and concur with a deep sense of knowing. This is incredible. It's an awakening to a new understanding, a revelation of the soul and its timeless journey through the experience of reincarnation."

"Yes, yes," she replied, "I too see a similar change in your features. I don't know how to explain it, and I don't think I want to try, but you're becoming Egyptian before my eyes. Your skin is darker and your hair is straight, black and cut to your shoulders. You're adorned with the gold and jewels of pharaonic royalty. Yes, I see it now, and I'm beginning to understand who you are, as well."

Raj affirmed their experience, adding, "Let's try to maintain our trance for there's much to discover. Keep breathing with me as we embrace. We're joined in a special way that has opened a portal to the past. Don't force the vision, and don't think about it. Just let it happen. Immerse yourself in the moment and look deeply into my eyes. Breathe with me. Follow the breath, follow the breath! Now, what do you see?"

Tamera's eyes closed and her voice became calm as she spoke with the muted intonations of a vanished tongue.

"I am a young woman named B'shepa, a handmaiden in the house of the great Pharaon. I serve the sister of the Pharaoh's consort and although I am treated well, my place in the household is clearly defined. I am sixteen years old and considered beautiful and full of life. Meekaba, my mistress, is old, no longer attractive, and very bitter. She watches her sister's power and position with envy, and mutters her disapproval under her breath. I must follow behind her and do her bidding. I live in her house and have few contacts beyond my duties. I am a slave. I accompany her wherever she goes, attending to her needs and desires." She paused as their breathing continued in a matched rhythm. Her eyes, still closed, moved behind their lids, like the rapid eye movement of a deep sleep.

"We regularly go to the royal residence where she is required to participate in the courtly activities of the Pharaon's family. The Pharaon is a god, but he is kind and gentle. For a god, he seems quite real. I prostrate before him with the others. I'm frightened to look upon him, but he allows us to rise and be ourselves."

She opened her eyes and said, "I have gone to a place that seems so familiar to me. Can this be true? Or, am I dreaming?"

"You're tapping into an ancient soul memory," Raj answered. "One in which you know the nature of who you were. It's O.K. to know this, to re-experience these memories bringing them into your current awareness. You are meant to have this knowledge. Perhaps you can blend these memories into who you are now, fulfilling the destiny that you began in the past. Let's continue to explore this."

She agreed and closed her eyes again, returning to the vision. "I am at the court of the Pharaon. There was a great feast, a celebration amongst the royal family. It has ended, and Meekaba, full with food and ale, has fallen asleep. Unrestrained by her demands, I wander through the royal house. I walk down a long corridor and enter a garden courtyard. It is bright, sunny and filled with fruit trees and exotic flowers of every hue and scent imaginable. I can hear the songs of birds. I can also hear the sound of children playing. I turn to observe the children. There are many children of different ages, all from the royal household. They are playing games and having fun. There is laughter and joy! I am happy to be with them. I recall how I was taken from my family at an early age and made to serve. I didn't get to play with other children; this was a great sadness for me.

"There, among the children, is an older boy. He is different from the rest, and appears to be about thirteen. He is beautiful to behold and has a majestic quality, an aura of refinement. He is dressed in the finest linen and wears gold armbands and necklaces. Several attendants stand close by, fanning him and carrying food and drink. He turns and looks my way and our eyes meet. I feel the power of his gaze, which takes my breath away. He calls for me from across the courtyard and sends one of his attendants to fetch me. The attendant tells me he is the eldest son of the great Pharaon, the Prince Ment'uhotep. He is considered to be a god, the heir to the dynasty. I go willingly, dutifully, as I've been called by a god. As I draw near to him I keep my eyes down to avoid his gaze. He calls out to me, asking my name. I shyly tell him, 'I am B'shepa, who serves the lady Meekaba.' He asks me to come with him and I obediently follow. I am led into a large room: the bed chamber of the young prince. The attendants tell me I have been blessed, as I have been chosen by a god. I am flattered and honored to be in his presence, but I don't know what to expect. I feel a great attraction to him and would gladly serve him. We are talking and holding hands. It is a very happy moment for me."

Still in trance, Tamera shuddered in Raj's arms. "I see Meekaba. She has entered into the Prince's chambers; she is upset. She scolds me for having wandered off from my duties. The young prince is timid in her presence and says nothing. She grabs me and leads me away. I am very sad and watch him as I leave the room. Our eyes are locked in contact.

"Some time passes, and I have been sent for by the young prince. I am excited and spend time preparing myself. Meekaba has consented to the request, as she cannot refuse, but she is upset and expresses her dissatisfaction. She berates me and threatens me in a jealous tantrum, but I am innocent and do not understand.

"I go to the prince. An escort is arranged and I am taken into the Pharaonic house by way of a secret entrance. When I arrive I am led to a special room filled with large pools of water where there are many women. There is much activity and the sound of many voices laughing and talking in a friendly, relaxed manner. They are engaged in the ritual bathing of the Pharaon's wives. I am taken among them and bathed and anointed in fragrant oils and flower essences. They make a great fuss over me and I am embarrassed by the attention. I am clothed in garments of the most magnificent kind: pure white cotton with gold threaded trim. I am adorned with jewels and broaches of gold and malachite, in the form of the goddess Isis and the winged symbol of Horus. A bevy of handmaidens care for me and apply the face paint of royalty. I am elevated by this treatment. It is a special moment for me, one of great dignity.

"At the appointed hour I am taken by a group of royal attendants and a contingent of priests with shaven heads to meet the prince. I am led to a garden surrounded by tall impenetrable hedges where the pleasing smell of exotic flowers fill the air with their scents. We are together in the garden; we are alone. He comes close to me and touches my hand. This feels good to me and I smile, looking away shyly. We sit on a gilded bench holding hands. He asks me if I'd like to come with him and I agree. We walk slowly to his bed chamber. We are surrounded by his attendants who are fanning us and burning a ritual *censer* filled with frankincense and myrrh. They disrobe me, but I am not ashamed. I lie down on the prince's divan and he approaches. The prince is young, but his passion is aflame. He takes me and I succumb, trying my best to please him. We are both inexperienced in the ways of love and it is finished quickly. They hurriedly take me away from his bed chamber.

"Raj," Tamera whispered, awakening from her vision, "Now I understand. It's finally becoming clear to me. The young prince, I see him. I see his face more clearly than ever. His face is in your face, your face in his. As I look at you, in trance, your face has changed to that of the prince. It's you! You were Ment'uhotep, the young heir to the great Pharaon. This is an incredible experience. Our lives touched then in the sweetest way, millennia ago. But I see more, as well."

"Please, don't stop. Go back and continue," Raj implored.

She quickly lapsed back into the trance. "My status seems uncertain; I am frightened. Meekaba, in a fitful rage over my visit to the prince has vowed to punish me. She is a bitter, vengeful woman twisted by hate. She is also very powerful. The ways of the inner court of the pharaonic family are filled with subterfuge, intrigue and deceit, and Meekaba has learned to play these games well. There is a code of ethics that must be followed by the royal family. The family members twist and manipulate the code to their own ends, driven by greed, jealousy and the desire for power and position. Meekaba has found out that the prince has asked to see me again. I am happy, but she is livid. She has become deranged by my relation to the prince, and is seething with venom for me. Her jealousy of my youth and beauty and the attention of Ment'uhotep has driven her insane. Her desire to castigate me knows no bounds. She cannot go against the prince's wishes because I am protected by that relationship, but her irrational jealousy and rage consume her.

"She is driven by her madness to a dreadful act. Knowing that she will be buried with her servants when the time comes to cross over to the land of the dead as was the custom of the royal family in accordance with pharaonic law, she commits the ultimate expression of her demented confusion. She takes her own life by poisoning herself with the venom of the deadly asp.

"She is dead. I am devastated and afraid for my life." Tamera was shaking and quivering in Raj's arms as she manifested the symptoms of a palpable terror from the events unfolding before her mind's eye.

"I am being led to the burial chamber in a royal funerary procession. A phalanx of attendants and priests carrying the ornate sarcophagus containing the mummified body of my mistress

CRUMBLING TEMPLE

marches slowly down the main causeway toward the necropolis. Observing the procession on a specially constructed platform is the royal family, including the prince. As I pass him, in a moment of panic I call out for his help. He can do nothing. The laws of the Pharaon will guide his every action. He looks at me and gestures weakly. We stare at each other horrified as I enter through the large stone edifice that forms the face of the funerary chamber. He is paralyzed with fear. I can see his helplessness and the longing in his eyes.

"The high priests intone the required chants recited from the sacred texts of the Book of the Dead. I hear their words and know that my fate is sealed. In my heart I long for the prince and his touch. I don't want to die, as I am in the full flower of my life. I call out to him and swear my love. I call out in the desperate cries of a condemned innocent. I call out that my heart and soul, my very ka, will always be with him. I cry out a last, despondent plea, as the massive, granite doors of the funerary chamber are shut and sealed in a final thunderous crash. Then, silence. It is too late, I have been buried alive."

She opened her eyes, now swollen with tears, and in a voice choked with emotion proclaimed, "I have found you again, my prince."

"Tamera, I believe you have." Raj responded affectionately. "We shared a young love so long ago, and now, here again, we share a new love. It's beautiful to know you and to understand the sacrifice that was made."

The trance began to subside, and their breathing became regular as they lay side by side on the warm, granite surface. In consummating their love, they discovered the ties that had bound their souls for thousands of years. Through their trance they had pierced the veil of memory penetrating to the core of their souls' experiences.

The last of the sun's rays filtered over the ruins as they left the

Temple of Abusir. They walked down the great stone causeway laughing and holding each other, leaving the crumbling pyramid behind them. They were transformed and renewed. A great love had brought their souls together, even after millennia. They crossed a threshold of understanding giving them knowledge of the immortality of their souls–a gift of wisdom that would be with them forever.

As they approached the farm, they could hear the sound of children playing. Omar saw Raj and Tamera and walked toward them at a relaxed pace. He was smiling and laughing as he spoke to Tamera in Arabic. She laughed and seemed to blush as she replied to him in the defensive manner that siblings might use.

"What did he say?" inquired Raj, hoping to pick up the inside track of their conversation.

"Oh, he said that we look like lovers and that he was happy to see us return so joyous from the temple."

"How could he know that?"

"He can tell, because it shows. We are a passionate people, and these things are always evident. He can see how happy we are. Happiness like this radiates on many levels."

"I see you have found Abusir quite engaging," Omar said to Raj.

"Shukran, thank you Omar for directing us to the temple. We had a wonderful time, one that I will never forget. Neither, I hope, will Tamera!"

"Ah, you are most welcome," he replied. "It gives me greater pleasure than you could know to see the smile on my lovely cousin's face. And the temple...ah, the temple is a place of magic and wonder for all who are fortunate enough to find themselves within her bounds. It is true grace, Insh' Allah. I had a feeling the temple was calling you. It is as if you have been guided here by some unseen force. These experiences have a way of causing themselves. It's always best if we can cooperate and participate willingly."

Crumbling Temple

They walked back to the main house, where the evening meal was being prepared. The cooking hearth was ablaze and the fragrant smell of fresh flat bread was wafting in the evening breeze. A large pot of couscous, a traditional grain dish, was cooking on the fire as Abdul prepared corn, peppers and roasted chicken. It grew dark quickly as they ate. The fire seemed to animate their faces as they sat exchanging stories and discussing local politics. In the distance, the lights of the city could be seen reflecting off the sandy haze, creating a dull glow in the night sky. Directly above, the first stars began to appear in the heavens, as the desert's heat dissipated into the cool evening air.

Omar stood up and had a brief conversation with Tamera. Raj waited patiently, sipping a bottle of warm ale. Omar turned to Raj and said, "I must go into town to meet some friends and pick-up some supplies. Tamera is very tired and will rest here, but you are welcome to come with me, if you wish."

Raj looked at Tamera, who was looking weary, and asked her affectionately, "Would you mind if I go with Omar? I still have some energy left."

"No, go ahead," she responded. "Omar has offered me his bed. It's an offer I cannot refuse. I'm very tired after a long and eventful day, and I'd like to get some sleep. Go with him, but come back later and stay here the night. You can join me in bed. I'll look forward to it."

Raj agreed and he and Omar drove off toward Cairo.

Keeper of Secrets

Chapter 5

THE MOON AND VENUS

Omar and Raj made their way out of the farm lands down a narrow dusty road that passed through the countryside into the outskirts of Cairo. Small villages gave way to rows of two-story mud-brick dwellings. The density of houses increased as they continued north, until blocks of six-story apartment buildings, back to back, stretched out in all directions. The roads were unpaved and everywhere a thick coating of dust gave a distinct gray hue to everything it settled on–and it settled on everything.

"Not many foreigners visit this part of Cairo," Omar said over the roar of the Jeep, downshifting into second as they approached a busy intersection. "It seems we are in need of some ingredients for tonight's festivities. I've been asked to take care of this small detail."

Raj nodded but was otherwise silent. They drove down unmarked roads turning often into darkened side streets and alleys. He didn't know where he was and felt disoriented.

"Where exactly are we?" he asked.

"Ah, this is just a neighborhood on the outskirts of Cairo. If you don't already know the way it's difficult to find. There are no street signs, and the people who live out here would never tell a foreigner how to find an address. They are very protective of their turf. It's an unspoken understanding."

"Well, that's real comforting," Raj responded sarcastically. "What did you mean when you said foreigners didn't visit here often?"

"Just that. Please, don't be concerned. Really, we'll be fine."

Raj could feel a tightening in his stomach as the Jeep slowed. The neighburhood seemed familiar, much like a tenement block in the inner city where he grew up. He was always wary of straying too far into unknown "hoods."

They stopped on the right side of the street at an intersection that looked almost identical to many other intersections seen along the way. The Jeep was double parked in front of a line-up of cars that all appeared to be from the forties and early fifties. Raj thought it remarkable to see so many vintage cars still on the road, a kind of vehicular mummification.

They both got out of the Jeep and stood momentarily in the street.

"I must go alone. Please, wait here." Omar said.

Raj nervously replied, "I'd really rather go with you, if that's OK."

"No," Omar said firmly, "wait here, please." He walked away briskly, without any further discussion, leaving Raj standing by himself in the middle of the street.

Raj took a deep breath and casually backed up to the Jeep, leaning and attempting to look at ease. A crowd gathered, as if clued in by radar or a sixth sense. The appearance of a stranger on their street attracted a small swarm of men, like bees responding to a hive intruder. First, a couple of young men in their teens approached. Then, several older men joined them. Soon Raj was surrounded by about fifteen men from the neighborhood, a few old men straggling into the crowd. He was in the center, pinned to the Jeep, and cut-off from flight by a semi-circle of live bodies, two to three deep. He was more than concerned and, in desperation, looked for Omar, who was nowhere in sight.

Raj smiled at no one in particular, looking around to scan the faces of the crowd. Each man peered at him from dark shadowy eyes; many had sunken cheek bones and pencil thin mustaches. These faces didn't smile back, but grimaced menacingly as they looked him over. The men murmured in hushed Arabic tones. He asked if anyone spoke English, but no one replied. Tension seemed to be mounting. Raj wondered whether he was violating their turf

The Moon and Venus

by being there. If only I had stayed in the Jeep, he thought, at least the glass and steel would have created some kind of barrier. He felt vulnerable but kept up a brave front.

An old man stepped out of the crowd and said something to Raj in Arabic. Not understanding, Raj said nothing. He searched his mind for the right phrase which might diffuse the agitated crowd. He looked up to the sky for inspiration and there it was, clear as a bolt of lightning.

Looking directly at the old man, Raj exclaimed with confident authority, as he pointed to the sky, "The Moon and Venus."

The crowd was stunned. They all looked up at the moon (almost full with Venus shining brightly nearby) at the same time, as if drawn by some mysterious force. Then, they looked at the old man, waiting for his response with hushed anticipation.

With a sense of revelation and insight, the old man spoke up with emphatic glee, "The Moon and Venoos," he said, pausing. Then he repeated it again, this time further exaggerating the 'oo' in Venus, "The Moon and Venooos!" He laughed and chuckled aloud, and with this pronouncement, the faces of the crowd lit up. Everyone relaxed and soon they were all repeating the line, just as the old man had said it. They continued laughing among themselves and then simply walked away. Within a moment, Raj was standing completely alone.

How interesting, he thought, puzzled but relieved at their departure. Just as in ancient times, people recognized the planets and stars and their influence. The moon and planets were woven into their lives through observation and myths. The simple mention of their presence conveyed a recognition that transcended the differences of language and culture.

Omar returned, walking up the street of nondescript apartment buildings, looking pleased with himself. "I hope I didn't keep you waiting long."

"Oh no, not at all. I was just hanging out," Raj said matter-of-factly.

Keeper of Secrets

"Good, then it's time to visit my cousin Ahmed. Now he knows how to work the sheesha. You're in for an interesting evening."

They got back into the Jeep and rode toward Giza.

Arriving at an aged, run-down tenement building they entered into its shadowy lobby. It was like entering a tomb instead of an inhabited apartment building. In the rear of the darkened portico was a stairwell silhouetted by the eerie glow of an old television set. Under the stairwell lived a poor squatter family bedded down for the night, enjoying an evening's entertainment. The space under the stairs was their living room, kitchen and bedroom.

"Be careful walking. There are no lights in the halls and no electricity to run them by. No one wants to pay for this amenity. Ahmed's uncle owns the building and lets him stay on the roof for free. That's where we're going; it's seven floors up."

Raj took out his butane lighter (their only source of light) and lit it. The floor landings were marked in Arabic numerals which came into view as they passed each landing. Occasionally, a sliver of light would pierce the darkness from under the door of an apartment, illuminating the crumbling white tiles of the worn pathway.

"You see," Omar continued, "these apartments have been lived in for generations. Once occupied, they are kept in families and passed on. It becomes very difficult to evict anyone or raise the rent because the apartments are rent controlled."

Breathing heavily from the vigorous, seven-story climb, Raj reached the last flight of stairs. The roof came into view, and with it, an enormous amount of concrete debris. Pile upon pile of broken concrete chunks littered the roof. At the far end of the roof was a small ramshackled one-room hut. It was made of old eroded planks with a patched tin roof.

The glow of an oil-burning lantern could be seen through an open window frame and through the cracks of the poorly joined lumber. It seemed that Ahmed's use of the roof required that he build his own shack out of whatever materials he could find. Judging from the bungalows that appeared on the surrounding rooftops, this was not an uncommon practice.

Omar called out to his cousin in a boisterous traditional Egyptian greeting. The hinged door of the one room shack opened wide, the twang of the stretched retention spring sounding an accompaniment to their melodious vocal exchange. Raj was happy to enter the place as a friend of a friend.

Omar introduced Raj, putting his arm around him saying, "This is my dear friend Raj from America. He is a welcome guest in my house; please welcome him into yours, Insh' Allah." Omar had vocally stressed the "America" part of the introduction as an important distinction, almost as if he were indicating an unusual "find." They considered the acquaintance of any world traveler a privilege, especially since they themselves were unlikely to travel beyond the boundaries of the Nile Valley, or even metropolitan Cairo. They savored information coming in from the "outside" and thirsted for the insights of these emissaries who had first-hand knowledge of the distant fast-paced world. Raj was honored by Omar's introduction and felt a strong bond developing between them.

"My cousin, I welcome you, and I welcome your friend. Please come in." Ahmed's voice was high-pitched and slightly nasal. He smiled broadly and opened the door.

Raj shook Ahmed's hand and thanked him for his welcome. The one-room dwelling was sparsely furnished and dominated by a king-sized bed. To the side of the bed was an old Persian rug and several pillows. Three other people were already seated on the rug. They smiled silently as Omar and Raj were directed to sit on some empty pillows. Ahmed and a woman friend sat on the bed. Together, they formed a non-symmetrical circle around the small room. Candles were lit on a small wooden table that also held a bottle of wine. Conversations started among the guests, who seemed to be well acquainted. They exchanged pleasantries with Raj in both English and Arabic, with Omar acting as translator.

Ahmed passed around a bottle of golden yellow Greek Retsina

wine and some paper cups. They drank a toast to their friendships, old and new. As the host, he began to speak, "Tonight our good friend and teacher, Omar, has brought a friend from afar, whom we welcome with open hearts. I hope that we may learn and grow together. Insh' Allah." After his brief benediction he brought out his sheesha and began preparing for the ritual.

A charcoal fire was lit in a tin coffee can by a young man in green Army fatigues, who, it was revealed, was AWOL from the Egyptian army. He had been hiding at Ahmed's for the past three weeks, and didn't seem to be concerned with his predicament. He proceeded to fire-up the coals with military precision. Another friend laid out a line of clay pipe bowls and prepared a mixture of habow and tobacco. Before long, there was an orderly line-up of packed bowls. Ahmed began smoking, providing a demonstration of his extraordinary lung capacity, puffing and exuding clouds of thick smoke.

The sheesha went around, passing from left to right in the circle. When it reached Raj, he exhaled to clear his lungs, and held the mouth piece firmly in his right hand as he began to draw upon it. The flavor of the smoke was earthy and strong with resins as it bubbled in vaporous blisters through the liquid of the pipe.

Everyone was relaxed and in good spirits. The room soon filled with translucent streams of billowous gray smoke. The Retsina moved amongst them as did the conversation, and they began to reveal a little about their lives and how they came to know Omar.

"Our friend Omar has been like a school to us." Ahmed continued, "He has shown us the way to open our hearts and minds."

Omar smiled proudly, saying, "You are too kind. I only offer friendship and guidance. I have been blessed with some knowledge of the inner self, and I teach about the pathways to reach that self."

"Omar understands the fine art of the Mota," said the soldier. "He has given us the means to go within where we can find our own truth."

"We are explorers, setting out on a long journey of discovery," interjected Rashid. "Only our ships are our minds, and the waters we set sail on are our thoughts and visions." Rashid was a young man in his early twenties, slender and quiet. His close-cropped, dirty blond hair was unusual for the dark-haired Egyptians.

"Well said, well said." Omar then continued: "Where the world of vision meets the world of dreams, we have found a place of enhanced perception. Upon entering that realm we experience the wonder of life's inter-relatedness. Soon, new dimensions of sight, sound and thought open up, revealing subtle realizations about the nature of the universe. The scale and scope of these thoughts cover any imaginable subject, from the insight that matter is an illusion of perception, to the revelation that the stars in our galaxy move as one conscious force through time and space. These insights become the maps of the inner planes we seek to explore. The Mota is the fabric from which we weave our sails to propel the explorations of these frontiers. We search for the source of knowledge from which the fountainhead of truth springs. It is there that we can learn about the mysteries of the universe, and it is there that we can come to know our essence, our very ka."

Raj was intrigued by the mention of the ka and wanted to pursue this line of thought, hopeful there might be additional information which would lead him to an ancient source. He had read that the teachings of the ancient priests might still be alive, handed down by an oral tradition unbroken through time. He also hoped that somehow this tradition had touched Omar, and that perhaps he was an emissary of one of the old wisdom schools. The thought fascinated Raj, but the conversation trailed off in a moment of introspection. Omar, deep in thought, looked off pensively through the open window into the dark Cairo night.

The sheesha fires faded, but the laughter and conversations continued. Ahmed announced that it was time to "commune with the muses" by playing Oriental music.

Oriental music is a classically developed Middle Eastern music deriving its uniqueness from the use of specific tonal scales, rhythmic cadences and unusual ethnic instrumentation. Its sounds are comprised of voice with accompaniment, sometimes including full orchestras. The instruments might consist of string sections with violins, ouds, hammer dulcimers, wind sections with oboes, flutes and *shinai*, and the percussion of dunbeks and tambourines.

Ahmed took great pleasure in the pronunciation of the word "oriental" with a strong emphasis on the final "tal" syllable. The Egyptians were very proud of their music as it played an important part in their lives. It spoke to their hearts and came from their experiences, coloring all aspects of their lives, permeating their homes, shops and streets. Ahmed spoke about oriental music, trying to explain it for Raj's benefit. He spoke with particular fondness of the music of Omm Al-Kalthoum, the greatest female oriental singer of memory. At the mention of her name everyone in the room exclaimed her greatness. Her music could be heard on many of the local radio stations. She had a special way with the characteristic glisses, arabesques and vocal escarpments that define the oriental sound.

Ahmed reached behind a dresser and pulled out two drums called *Dumbeks* one made of ornately patterned ceramic and one of metal. They had an hour-glass shape with one end open and the other end covered in a tautly pulled goat-skin head. The soldier and Ahmed were the first to play. They began with a slow repetitious beat. Everyone was drawn into its spell as the evening's stillness was pierced by the solemn ceremonial beat.

Then an *Oud* was brought out. The Oud is a medieval, fretless six-stringed instrument that closely resembles a lute. This Oud was beautifully crafted from oak and spruce and had a fret board of black ebony with mother of pearl inlay. Its sound hole was fitted with a delicately carved lattice, Islamic in motif, and its tuning pegs were made of carved rosewood.

Raj raised his hand and volunteered to play the Oud. To everyone's surprise, he began to play the instrument with natural skill. He had played both rock and jazz guitar since he was young, and

The Moon and Venus

was happy to be putting his years of practice to good use. He played some of the oriental "riffs" he had been hearing on the radio, following the rhythmic cadences of the Dumbek players. Raj had the gift of perfect pitch and a remarkable tonal memory.

His trained ear served him well, as he was able to transpose what he was hearing into useful musical expressions. He was surprised at how easy it was to play the Oud, an instrument he had never played before. Within a few measures, he had learned the basic oriental scales with their rhythmic complements and was able to improvise in a proficient, creatively-rich manner.

He soon felt a surge of energy in his fingers. They seemed to be driven by an intuitive ability that welled up from somewhere deep within. He began to play like never before, with a level of skill that surprised him, as he looked down to see his fingers flying across the fret board. It was as if some other-worldly force had taken over. He had become a channel expressing a deep understanding of oriental musical. He easily played complex scales and arpeggioes combining basic musical elements to produce a variety of sounds.

Raj could feel there was a special energy at work. It supported and inspired him. Everyone was feeding their energy into the music. The experience was opening doors to new worlds of perception that transcended his normal aural senses. Just when the music seemed as though it could go no higher, it would build again. Time after time, the music climaxed in resounding crescendos.

It was at an apex, in the midst of the ongoing fervor, that Raj did the unexpected. He began to sing in the forceful, plaintive cry of an Islamic *Muezzin*, something he had never done before. The vocal display of his perfectly pitched, three-octave voice, modulating with astonishing accuracy and inflection, caught everyone by surprise. In that moment, he touched the soul of the oriental. He had penetrated to the core of their music.

Omar cried out, "Yes! yes!" while the faces of Ahmed and the others revealed astonishment and approval.

With Raj's emotional display, the pace and vigor of the music intensified. Everyone was caught up in the frenzy of the moment. Then, Fatima, Ahmed's friend, jumped from the bed, her passion aflame as she raised her arms above her head and began to clap to the beat, pounding the floor with her feet in a deliberate, hip-swinging cadence. She was a seductive woman dancing provocatively in a room filled with young men in the prime of their youth. She moved around the room, dancing circles around each of them, drawing them into her excited state with pirouettes and other subtle movements. Her long black hair flew freely about her shoulders, and she trailed a colorful scarf as an accent to her movements. Each crescendo carried her deeper into trance. She was soon glistening with sweat which dripped down her cheeks, carrying the kohl from her eyes in erratic black traces. The musky smell of patchouli oil and her sweat filled the room. It was a wild spectacle as she vied for everyone's affections which they lavishly showered on her with cheers of encouragement.

Ahmed could no longer contain himself as he watched Fatima parade excitedly before his friends. This was more than he could bear; an affront to his conservative Islamic upbringing. He rose up and forcefully grabbed her by the arm, pulling her down to the bed. She recoiled from him, hurt by his actions. The ensuing argument startled the entire group, breaking the sacred mood of the gathering. The music abruptly stopped as harsh words were exchanged between them. Raj didn't get a translation but didn't need one either. It was clear that Ahmed was angry, as if an unspoken code of ethics had been broken.

Raj observed the incident with a detached regard. He was still in a state of high transport from the intense musical experience. Although he was quickly brought down to the moment, he was dazed by the suddenness of it all and looked to Omar for help.

Omar was quick to react to the situation. Rather than get involved he made the move to leave, making excuses about the time and other pressing engagements. Besides, they were all tired and the evening had been outstanding, overall. Omar was graceful in his approach, and he and Raj quickly said good-bye and left.

They were well into the street when Omar spoke again, saying, "That was incredible, wonderful, what an experience! I couldn't have hoped for more. Never mind Ahmed and Fatima; that was just a lover's quarrel. But the music, the joy of it, the bliss! This is what we refer to as *Ishtah Alaek*. This means, literally, the cream off the top of the milk. It is a metaphor we use for the very, very best. The sweetest most desirable experience or thing is this Ishtah Alaek. I tell you, my friend, we definitely crossed over tonight."

"Ah! I'm walking on air. That was very sweet," Raj replied.

"Yes, we went to a place of harmony and freedom," Omar continued. "Bringing an exalted awareness through music is a holy task and a great blessing. Thank you for your contribution. You sounded like you were channeling the old soul of a skilled Muezzin. I was amazed! And your Oud playing! Where did you learn to play like that?"

"I just opened up and let it flow. It came through me like water. No...like the sweet cream, like Ishtah Alaek!"

"Kways, good!" Omar said, as he climbed into the Jeep and started the engine. They quickly drove south, out of town. "We have, you know, the potential to reach beyond our capabilities, but this requires an extraordinary set of circumstances–some training, presence of mind, a great deal of heart, a supreme effort, and something else far more important." He paused as they veered hard left, his concentration shifting momentarily to the road. "And that is grace."

"How do you mean?" asked Raj, weary from the evening's festivities but interested in the trend of Omar's thought.

"When we are striving and are applying ourselves, be it in art, science, or business, we make progress toward our goals, but encounter limits in the rate and pace of our development. In most cases, long years are required to develop even modest capabilities in most disciplines. But I have experienced breakthroughs that are far beyond the expression of natural abilities. It has been suggested that we carry deep within us memories, knowledge and talents that are a part of our soul's remembrance. These resources have been developed over innumerable lives and can be accessed. But you may ask, how can that be done?

"We can only access this knowledge by invoking the assistance of a guiding force that comes from outside of ourselves. This force is the power of grace. Grace is the beneficent energy that shifts the consciousness beyond the limits of its capabilities. Without grace, there can be no significant leap in our natural development. Grace is a noble force that is divine in nature. When we have prepared ourselves, and only when we make the requisite call, can we receive this grace.

"Tonight you have experienced 'call and response'. It is the basis of our worship. We worship all that is exalted and good in ourselves, in each other, and in our universe. We worship through communion in sound and rhythm. We send out the call and, if our mind is clear and free from distraction, and our heart is true and filled with love, we receive a response. That response is the flow of the beneficent energy called grace. We can receive this grace as an expansion of the capacity of our hearts and minds, resulting in a transcendent experience, such as tonight. Unfolding as we played, it expressed our divine nature in a way that I can only describe as–bliss.

"It is there that we touch the great universal essence. Once we have tasted this, we can never abandon the quest. We are compelled to continue the process, perfecting the channel of contact with the source. Not only for ourselves, but to anchor this benevolent energy for the benefit of all. I have dedicated my life to this."

By the time they reached Abusir it was early in the morning. Omar showed Raj into the main house and went to sleep outside. Raj found Tamera sleeping soundly in bed and quietly crawled in, nestling up to her warm, soft body. She sighed and whispered that she had been waiting for him. They both drifted off, entwined in each other's arms.

The Moon and Venus

By late the next morning they were up and about. It was hard to sleep in, especially with the farm noises. The roosters had been up crowing since dawn and could not be ignored. Still, Raj had a good night's sleep and was affectionately awakened by a gentle kiss from Tamera. She was already preparing a breakfast of eggs and potatoes. The smell of strong coffee filled the air as he made his way to the kitchen. The brilliant morning sunlight streamed in through the open windows casting a golden glow on the room's baked clay walls.

"Sabah al-khair, my love," Tamera said to Raj, as he splashed water on his face from a wash basin positioned in front of an east facing window. *"Ahwah, masboutah?"* she suggested, offering Raj the traditional cup of morning coffee with sugar–just right.

"*Masbut*, and good morning to you too!" he replied, pulling her toward him from behind and embracing her tightly, "you are masbut, you are ishtah, Ishtah Alaek!"

She laughed at his attempt at an Arabic complement, but was flattered just the same, and turned wrapping her arms around his shoulders, giving him a long, passionate kiss. "You are a real charmer, Raj. Ishtah Alaek, indeed! Sounds like you've been paying attention to the local language. I like that!"

Raj was pleased with himself and his ability to pick up an important piece of the local language, but he was even more pleased with his budding romance with Tamera, whom he found even more beautiful in the waxing morning light.

Omar soon entered the farm house in good cheer. They had coffee and made plans to spend the day together exploring some of the surrounding monuments that could only be reached from Abusir by a Jeep ride through the desert. The timing seemed perfect. Raj knew in his heart he was being guided on his journey. He looked forward to a private tour of the surrounding monuments and a chance to see the ancient fingerprints of a once vibrant culture, now obscured by shifting desert sands.

Keeper of Secrets

Chapter 6

STEP PYRAMID

Omar gave parting instructions to Abdul and with Raj and Tamera drove off through the fallow fields at the outer edge of the Nile Valley. Leaving the known road, they sliced a virgin path into smoothly blown sand and entered the immense Sahara. The rolling dunes unfolded beneath them like a heaving ocean's liquid terrain. Cresting their first dune, they saw all that was green, good and full of life disappear behind them. In the distance, they could see a faint outline against the horizon, a pattern of steps rising to a flattened apex–the Step Pyramid of the Necropolis of Saqqara.

Omar drove directly toward the Step Pyramid, which could be seen pale ochre against the clear blue morning sky. The Jeep bounced as it rolled over each ripple of sand. He turned on his tape player and turned up the volume on Beethoven's Ninth Symphony. The Jeep seemed to keep perfect time with the music, rolling over the dunes in sync with the shifting symphonic score.

"I love riding in the desert with classical music," Omar said, clearly in his element as he strained to keep the Jeep in an upright position. Raj held on to the support handles and Tamera held onto the back of Raj's seat. Omar floored the accelerator with the expected result, launching the vehicle in dips and dives that shuddered to the ground in a jarring, bronco-kicking manner.

"What's the chance this thing could flip over?" Raj asked.

"*Mafesh mushkilah,*" Omar yelled through the sound of the over-amped music and the roar of the fully-torqued engine. "No problem."

They rolled through the desert forging through the bleak terrain. The hilly rises blended one into another, but Omar knew the way, skillfully navigating around the shifting contours of the dunes.

Keeper of Secrets

On each rise they could see the outline of the pyramid coming into focus, the details of its individual stones becoming more sharply pronounced with each passing mile.

They turned into a *wadi* (dry gully) and came upon a curious monument seemingly out of place in a landscape filled with some of the great wonders of the ancient world. Before them was the Dromos, a monument erected to honor several Greek philosophers. These statues were lined up in a semi-circular arrangement sheltered by a simple plastered wall and roof. Omar paid little attention to them as they cruised by. The philosophers were alone in a ravine separated from other monuments. All Raj could do was give a parting salute as they drove past and over the next ridge into Saqqara, the temple complex of the third dynasty Pharaoh Djoser.

Remarkable for its complexity and dimensions, Saqqara contained an astounding number of tombs, temples and pyramids spanning Egyptian history. Its antiquity made it holy as each successive pharaoh prepared a place next to the great ones, the ancient god-kings, who were holy even in their own times. Slowly, over millennia, the subsequent addition of tombs, *mastabahs* and other funerary monuments caused a steady expansion of the necropolis.

When first built by the high priest, scholar and architect, Imhotep, the Step Pyramid was the first of its kind in both design and execution. Its construction ushered in an age of extraordinary pyramid-type monument-building that peaked in Giza with the great pyramids of Khufu (Cheops), Khaph-Ra (Chephren) and Menkaure (Mycerinus). Although the Saqqara pyramid was always visible above the desert plains, the tombs and temple complexes had been buried in the sand until early this century. Excavation has been an ongoing project, as more and more of the site is uncovered from thousands of years of blowing sand.

"We must go to see my good friend Dr. Rashid Ali," Omar declared. "He is an old Nubian colleague of mine who has worked for the Egyptian Antiquities Organization for many years. He has been stationed at the Saqqara site for the last ten years and is always aware of the latest findings. We have spent many nights together interpreting the hieroglyphs found in some of the tombs. It is there that important teachings were recorded and left for posterity by the ancient priests. Much was written in obscure symbology, but Dr. Ali is considered an expert in the field. He reads the hieroglyphs fluently and with a keen sense of their meanings. Besides, he is a wonderful man, always congenial, a truly delightful person."

"Great," Raj offered. "It will be exciting to meet someone who lives and breathes Egyptology. Anyone who can read hieroglyphic symbols like an open book must have some interesting stories to tell."

Raj was awed by the immensity of the the step Pyramid. The outer walls of the complex extended almost two thousand feet from north to south and one thousand feet from east to west. It was difficult to conceive that the whole area was almost completely buried for the last five thousand years. The Complex of Djoser was flanked by other pyramids and temples, including those of the Goddess Sekhmet and the tombs of previous Pharaohs with names such as Teti, Meriruka, Ankh-ma-hor, Unis, Userkaef, Nefer, Nefer-her-ptah, Ni-ankh-hotep, Khnum-hotep, Ptah-hotep, Akhet-hotep and others. Their tombs covered an area of four square miles and spanned the entire reign of pharaohs from the First to the Thirty-First Dynasties and beyond.

They drove around the temple area, continuing past the Pyramid of Teti to the offices of the Inspector of Antiquities. The small one-story mud-brick building was dwarfed by the surrounding monuments. Its simple construction next to the complex stone work and classic proportions of the adjacent temples and pyramids provided a stark contrast. The reception area of the office was dominated by several maps, including a detailed map showing the outlines of the archeological excavation sites at Saqqara. It was covered in multi-colored pins, but without a legend to tell what the pins meant. Another map showed the Nile Valley and the archeological sites of both Upper and Lower Egypt, while a third map showed the political borders of the modern state. On a wall above the reception counter was a picture of President Hosni Mubarak, framed and surrounded by a red, white and blue bunting, along with a large-faced clock frozen at three-thirty, and several small, wall-mounted oscillating fans. The fans put out a welcome intermittent breeze which provided some relief to the oven-like feeling of the office interior. Several wooden chairs were placed against one wall next to an aged soft drink dispensing machine.

Omar spoke briefly to the man at the front desk, who quickly left the room, and then went over to the soda machine. After sizing it up, he deposited some change and produced three ice-cold colas which were quickly consumed.

Within a few minutes, a corpulent blue-black Nubian in a white *gelabia* appeared, smiling effusively and shouting his greeting toward Omar.

"Dr. Rashid Ali," Omar answered, "Please meet my dear cousin Tamera and our American friend Raj." Dr. Ali was jovial and seemed genuinely pleased to meet them, shaking Raj's hand vigorously and giving Tamera a kiss on each cheek.

Dr. Ali had come to Cairo with a wave of Nubians that had migrated north after the construction of the High Dam at Aswan. Literally hundreds of thousands of Nubian villagers were displaced by the rising waters of Lake Nasser, one of the largest man-made lakes on earth. Along with villages, countless temples and other important archeological sites were inundated by the backed-up Nile. Most of these sites were lost forever, but some of them were rescued and brought to higher ground.

Among them was a colossal Ramses II temple–the Temple of Abu Simbel–which was sliced from a mountain by a team of archeologists from UNESCO and moved sixty feet above the original site. This was accomplished with an accuracy and precision that allowed a shaft of light to pierce one hundred and eighty feet into the temple entrance at the exact moment of the sunrise on the vernal and autumnal equinoxes. At that moment, statutes of Ramses and his queen were illuminated with awe-inspiring effectiveness just as the temple had been designed to do in its original location.

With the displacement of many Nubians and the resultant hardships, a select few were given plum assignments within various governmental agencies. Dr. Ali, who was studying Egyptology in Cairo and doing his field research at the Nubian sites soon to be immersed, was given a job with the EAO and was eventually placed at Saqqara. It was a wise choice, because Dr. Ali proved to be an extraordinary scientist with a profound understanding of some of the most important excavation sites in Egypt.

"Sabah al-khair," intoned Dr. Ali. "Such a delight to meet you. You have come to see me on an especially good day." He was excited but maintained a dignified calm. "Omar, I was actually thinking of you earlier. You see, my most recent excavations have yielded very important information. Something I'm sure you will want to know about. I can hardly contain my excitement."

"Please, tell us more, Dr. Ali," Omar implored.

"Well, as I explained to you in our last visit, the entire north side of the Djoser complex has long been buried under the sands, perhaps for most of the last four or five thousand years. We had a feeling that under the rubble were significant archeological discoveries that might contain important hieroglyphs. We surmised from our earlier work in the south section that the north section of the complex might contain new information about the creator of the temple complex, the great master builder Imhotep. We only recently received the go-ahead to commence our excavations. But please, before I get too involved, let's go to my office for some refreshments."

Omar agreed and they followed Dr. Ali down the narrow hallway toward his office. They walked in single file, because the hallway was lined on each side, from top to bottom, with packed bookshelves. The shelves contained an assortment of textbooks, note-

Keeper of Secrets

books, rolled-up maps, various small statues, and piles of stones inscribed with hieroglyphics. They were all covered with thick dust. There was little organization to the stacks, which probably contained a fortune in ancient artifacts and, even more precious, the working data for some of the most significant archaeological finds from the last fifty years. What extraordinary revelations might be buried, not only in sand, but in the detailed research notes describing those hieroglyphic writings, carefully copied and translated. The accumulated knowledge of thousands of years of Egyptian civilization, retrieved but still hidden, lined the walls as they walked down the corridor to Dr. Ali's office.

In the office, every available square inch of space where it was possible to store or stack something was in use, except for Dr. Ali's chair. His desk (which was completely covered with stacks of papers and assorted odds and ends) and two guest chairs were also crammed into the room. Actually, devoid of its shelves, crates, stacked boxes and furniture, the room would have been more than adequate. However, there was hardly enough room for the four of them to fit, much less to sit. Omar and Tamera sat in the available chairs, while Raj leaned precariously on the most stable stack of boxes, which he somehow managed to balance against the nearest bookshelf.

Crammed onto the shelves was an astonishing collection of antique books, papyri, and peculiar stone tablets covered with hieroglyphs of exceptional quality. Each had a story to tell, a meaning that revealed its origin, its author, its purpose, and perhaps an underlying metaphor that was encoded in writing and symbology, for the trained eye to read. Raj realized that, to make it into Dr. Ali's office, these objects had to have special significance, because he certainly had his choice of artifacts.

The saving grace of Dr. Ali's cluttered office was the exceptional view from his office window which looked out directly to the Step Pyramid, its stony face hard against the cerulean blue sky, its graduating levels framed perfectly in the plain window.

Step Pyramid

Dr. Ali was sweating profusely and regularly mopped his brow with a white handkerchief that he periodically pulled out from under his gelabia. Since he kept his panoramic window sealed shut for security reasons, the temperature soon soared in the stuffy room. Despite the heat, Dr. Ali called for his assistant to bring coffee. He also managed to turn on a large wood and cane bladed ceiling fan which created a paltry breeze.

Within moments, the office attendant returned with four demitasse cups of dark coffee. He skillfully slipped into the office and slid between the chairs to deposit the tray on Dr. Ali's desk.

"You know," Dr. Ali began, "these are most fascinating times for Egyptologists. On the one hand, we have been taught that the chronology of the Pharaonic dynasties has been well figured out and provides us with a complete picture of the history of Egypt. On the other hand, there have always been pieces of the historical puzzle missing, and this has caused some Egyptologists to question the accepted chronological models. The problem is that we haven't found reliable proof for either theory. Even with advanced scientific dating techniques, like radio isotope carbon-14 dating, we can never be sure of the original dates for the construction of most of the older monuments. You see, the stones simply cannot be dated, even if they were marked with a chisel. Carbon-14 dating uses organic matter, such as the burnt remains of a nearby fire, to determine the general date of origination. The stones themselves are silent! We cannot tell when the stones were put into place, especially where older stones from previous monuments were used, as was often the case. Proving dates is a very tricky procedure, often open to various interpretations.

"Of course, from an academic standpoint, and from the standpoint of the government and the EAO, this questioning of the dynastic time line is heretical and could easily ruin one's career as an Egyptologist. You can imagine there haven't been many of us who have been willing to step forward to present new ideas or advance our interpretations of history, no matter how appealing or presumably logical they might be. However, it is the missing pieces of the puzzle that I have been seeking, and I believe that some of this puzzle has now been revealed through the latest findings at Djoser's Temple. We finally have the proof that has eluded us since the beginning of the modern era of excavations, and we can now dispute the currently accepted timelines. With our revised interpretations, we can throw out the old chronological understanding about the history of the Egyptian civilization, and with it our conceptions about the history and origins of humankind."

Clearly, Dr. Ali was referring to something that had shaken his own understanding of the subject and caused him to question the premise that he had devoted much of his academic life to proving and supporting.

"Please Doctor, I must know more!" Omar interjected excitedly.

Raj and Tamera were spellbound as they listened to Dr. Ali's story. Raj noticed a slight edge of tension in his voice. Despite his genuine excitement, he spoke with an inflection suggesting nervousness. Perhaps there was a lot more to the story than he was revealing.

"Our academic scholars, those main-stream Egyptologists," Dr. Ali continued, "have become quite smug in the assumptions gleaned from their so-called 'empirical' data. Much of the story of our ancestors, who for hundreds of generations have walked the Nile Valley, is yet to be told. Much is still buried under the sands. A thousand Egyptologists working night and day would still take centuries to uncover what has been buried over the millennia. And even then, what of the translations, what of the interpretations?

"These hieroglyphs, especially the older third and fourth dynasty writings, are composed of complex pictograms written to convey thoughts not only through the outer symbol, but in other, more subtle, ways. Each glyph can be read as part of a greater glyphic word, or it can be read as a root word. Each glyph has within it a subtle meaning that describes a deeper truth, especially when read with the root-glyphs of other adjoining hieroglyphs. These will then reveal a separate meaning underlying the outer mundane communication. The ancient scribes and priests were masters of this skill. They were able to encode their language with hidden meanings that were decipherable only to the initiated, those with 'eyes to see'. In this way, they were able to disseminate sacred insights without fear that their instructions would fall into the wrong hands–the hands of those who would abuse the hekau, or sacred words of power."

"Dr. Ali," asked Omar, "is it possible to see these hieroglyphs? It would be useful for us to take a look at them. These writings, unseen for so long, have a special vibration created by the original authors. They have left a little of their magic in the stone, imbued it with their ka, as it were, which has been preserved by their entombment. This would be a special favor for me, my friend. Insh'Allah."

"Yes, of course. This can be arranged. In fact, I can take you there now."

They drank the last of their coffee and got up to leave. Raj inquired about the books and artifacts strewn about the office. Dr. Ali replied, chuckling to himself, that all that came with the territory and that he was fond of the clutter, having made, in his mind, a detailed accounting of all of the elements of his collection categorized according to his current interests. On the way out, Dr. Ali grabbed a canteen and filled it with water, fresh and cold from the office cooler. He slung it over his shoulder along with a bag containing a flashlight, a camera, a notebook and a pen. In his world, he was heading for work.

The transition into the blazing glare of the mid-day Saharan sun caused a momentary blindness, prevented by the quick donning of brimmed hats and sunglasses. The group proceeded to walk the short distance to the Step Pyramid, despite the heat, so they could see more of the Saqqara complex, especially those areas currently under excavation. Dr. Ali assumed the role of their walking tour guide, explaining the nuances of the temple complex as could only a seasoned Egyptologist who had uncovered the ancient monuments on his knees with a toothbrush.

"You are now standing on over five thousand years of history," he remarked, "and what you see only hints at the complex maze of passageways and funerary chambers that lie below, hidden from view. The Step Pyramid complex covers thirty-seven acres and the surrounding wall is almost a mile around. The pyramid itself has six tiers, although excavations have shown that it originally had four. When it was completed, it stood over two hundred feet high and was covered with Tura limestone, polished to a smooth and shiny finish. It must have been a magnificent sight when first completed, awe-inspiring and visible for miles around. The outer covering of polished limestone is gone of course, the limestone face pilfered to build other monuments, mosques and houses. Sometimes they just burned or crushed the stone and plowed the limestone dust into the fields as fertilizer. Such a waste, such a pity." Dr. Ali was clearly pained by the deliberate destruction and recycling of these monuments.

"The outer walls of the temple area had fourteen false doors," Dr. Ali described, "but only one true door, located on the southeast side of the complex. It is here that the dig first began in 1925, when the sands of the south court were cleared. Now, we are walking into the southern courtyard, which is as it first appeared to the eminent Egyptologists, Cecil Firth and Jean-Phillipe Lauer, when they uncovered it and began to explore the tombs. They also had the good sense to rebuild the colonnade entrance, which gives you a sense of its former glory. Notice, on your left, the stone friezes depicting cobras on the top of the first building."

They walked north toward the Step Pyramid, a mammoth and impressive structure. Even from far away, the pyramid's antiquity was accentuated by the mounds of debris that had accumulated on the tops of the tiers.

They proceeded around the east side of the pyramid, past the ceremonial Sed court, to an area just to the north, which turned out to be an active dig site. The morning dig had already been completed, and the excavation workers had already left for the afternoon break. It was their job to clear the sand and lay out the string grid lines that were the basis of the excavation records. The afternoon siesta was a necessity in desert archeological work, as the sun grew too hot for effective physical labor. Afterward, in the late afternoon and early evening, the presiding dig leader would write up the day's excavation notes, categorizing the finds and making observations. It was only during the early hours of the day that anyone was on-site doing the actual digging.

The desolation of the site gave it an eerie feeling. There was a strange silence punctuated by the intermittent whistle of errant breezes slicing through unseen fractures in a crumbling stone wall. Dr. Ali made his way through a cordoned off area that was being carefully worked in a marked grid of varying layers. Each day's work was drawn and photographed to preserve the exact location of any wall foundations or artifacts uncovered. Within the limits of the yellow-stringed excavation area was a half-uncovered doorway that opened to blackness.

Dr. Ali invited them to enter the dig site and follow his footsteps. He made a bee-line to the stone orifice that yawned from out of the sand and debris. When they assembled at the doorway to the tomb, Dr. Ali explained, "You must realize that this tomb has just been opened. Please be very careful, for there is considerable debris on the ground. Please, do not touch anything, especially the walls, as the oils from your hands might damage the delicate pigments of the hieroglyphs you are about to see."

He paused and passed around his canteen, which was gladly accepted. Before entering the tomb, Dr. Ali took out his camera and took a picture of the group at the entrance. He put the camera on automatic and propped it up on a nearby stone wall so that he could get a picture of everyone together. Taking out his flashlight, he continued his explanation. "The first known hieroglyphic wall writings were found at the Saqqara necropolis in the pyramid of the fifth dynasty Pharaoh Unis. Before that, no hieroglyphic writings were found in any of the earlier tombs.

"Why that is so, is a mystery. However, in the pyramid of Unis were discovered the famous Pyramid Texts, which are comprised of over two hundred magical spells composed to protect the soul of the pharaoh in the afterlife. These hieroglyphs were cut into the stone and filled with a blue paste made of ground-up minerals, which gave them a lasting clarity. These texts have given us important insights into the religious practices of the early Egyptians.

"What you are about to witness is an exciting and important find. It is the first written tomb record of the early Old Kingdom, dated to the time of Djoser in the third dynasty, which pre-dates the Great Pyramids of Giza. The reason for the significance of all this will become apparent. Please follow me closely."

There was a moment of hesitation mixed with some understandable apprehension, as is usually felt prior to plunging into the unknown. The fact that the tomb had just been opened excited Raj, but he also had some trepidation connected with violating its sanctity. Perhaps an ancient malevolent curse might result from such a transgression.

They all stayed closely behind Dr. Ali, who was followed by Omar and Tamera, with Raj taking up the rear. Slowly, they made their way into the tomb entrance, following Dr. Ali's every move, stooping low as they entered because the sand at the doorway had not been completely cleared. Immediately, Dr. Ali turned on his flashlight and stopped for a moment to allow his eyes to adjust to the darkness. He aimed his flashlight deep into the corridor. They could see that it extended for quite a ways and appeared to branch off into an indeterminate number of doorways. They were awed by the perfectly aligned masonry that seemed, because of perspective, to shrink in the distance, as rows of impeccably placed stones receded toward the vanishing point. They continued into the pitch-black, granite encased hallway, but there was not much to see. Nor was there much to fear except the remote possibility that a cave-in might entomb them. The air was stale, probably much of the same air that was sealed into the tomb at the time of the Pharaoh Djoser. They continued down the tunnel-like corridor, passing several rooms that Dr. Ali indicated were empty.

"What were these rooms used for?" Tamera inquired.

"Truthfully," Dr. Ali confessed, "I am uncertain at the moment; we are still studying this problem."

The only sounds they could hear were the sounds of their own footsteps and their labored breathing echoing off the polished granite walls. Behind them, light from the entrance receded to a faint glow, giving them the feeling that they were being swallowed up. The outside world of daylight seemed further and further away. They continued walking briefly pausing at each open doorway to illumine the interior of the chambers which revealed–absolutely nothing.

They paused again as Dr. Ali explained in a soft, clear and rational voice, "When I first entered the tomb, you can imagine my excitement; I was literally shaking with anticipation. Actually, I was somewhat overwhelmed by the magnitude of the place–such a long a corridor, so many chambers to explore. As my team and I made our initial inspection of each of the rooms, I became concerned, even disappointed, at what we had found, as room after room was completely empty. Unlike other mastabahs and tombs we have excavated, where there was usually an assortment of sarcophagi, mummified remains, scarabs, Ushabti, clay pots, statues, jewelry or some other form of artifact, these rooms were bare. Of course, we expected that they were probably looted several thousand years ago, but that would still not account for the complete bareness of the rooms. Even the greediest of grave robbers left some objects or fragments of objects that they considered to be worthless. Usually they were overlooked or discarded in favor of something more valuable. Things containing gold and precious gems, easy to unload on the black market, were always taken. But

KEEPER OF SECRETS

to an archaeologist, even worthless fragments and leftovers are invaluable and can be pieced together to tell the story of what went on when the objects were created and put to use. This is, after all, what our science is about. These rooms must have had some ceremonial purpose, but I am unclear as to what that might have been. Even the walls were bare, but this was anticipated and in keeping with the findings of other monuments of the Third and Fourth Dynasties.

"The initial survey, which was a cursory look into each unsealed room, observing and recording its interior, went on systematically for two days. An ongoing video record of the exploration was made for future reference. We determined that there were twenty-two chambers along the main corridor, all with entrances on the right side of the gallery. We went down to the end of the hall, which finally dead-ended, and were returning to the entrance. About halfway back, in room eleven, one of my sharp-eyed assistants observed something that seemed unusual. Although we found the room void of any artifacts or writings, we noticed that the rear wall appeared to be different from the rest of the room. We noticed an odd seam about a third of the way out from the left-hand side of the wall as we approached. Then we discovered that there was a gap that could not be accounted for in the normal construction of the wall. Upon closer examination, we observed another gap in an adjoining section of the wall approximately one meter from the first gap. Both of these gaps, however slight, were perfectly straight, from floor to ceiling, and were incongruous relative to the staggered placement of other stones in the wall." Dr. Ali paused to catch his breath. He took a swig of water from his canteen, wetting his mouth parched by the old, stale air.

"Please go on," implored Omar.

"Perhaps it would be better if I just showed you."

They followed Dr. Ali down the long corridor past several more rooms. He turned right and walked into a room with a distinctly marked number written on the entryway threshold. It was the number eleven written in Arabic numerals with day-glow pink colored chalk.

The chamber appeared to be about five meters deep and about three meters wide. The ceiling was low and could be touched by an outstretched hand. The walls were constructed of blocks of finely dressed, smooth red granite. Each block was at least one meter long and one-half meter wide and was laid in perfect symmetry to the block above. At the rear of the chamber Dr. Ali outlined the gaps in the wall by passing the beam of his flashlight swiftly down the cleft lines separating the stones.

"You see, this is what we first saw when we began to examine the room. We knew it was different from the other chambers we explored." He pulled a box of matches out of his pocket and struck one against the side of the box. It ignited in a burst of light temporarily casting grotesque shadows around the room. They all drew close to observe the flickering flame as Dr. Ali placed the lit match up to the gap. "Watch closely; watch the direction of the flame," he suggested.

Faint air movement caused the flame to veer outward away from the wall. "This indicates there is another source of air, and perhaps a room, behind this wall," Dr. Ali asserted. "But that is not all. After careful examination, we began to look for some way to penetrate the wall. We pushed on it every possible way. I thought it might be sealed by a granite plug, such as those found blocking the entrances to the Great Pyramids of Giza. My crew and I spent a considerable amount of time exploring all the possibilities when I carelessly dropped my pocket knife. It fell to the floor, blade first. But, instead of sticking into the thick dust, it barely penetrated and bounced off the ground with a pinging sound. I quickly bent down and began to brush away the dust until I uncovered a strange grooved stone. After stopping to photograph and catalog the find, I proceeded to move and manipulate the stone in every possible way. Finally, with all my strength, and some luck, it miraculously started to give. I succeeded in raising the stone about ten centimeters when we heard an audible thunk somewhere beneath the floor." As he was telling the story, Dr. Ali grabbed hold of the grooved part of the stone and pulled up on it strenuously. Suddenly a distinct sound was heard.

"Now, watch this," he said, as he leaned hard against the left section of the wall. Slowly it began to move, with a scraping, grinding sound. The wall section was turning on a central pivot, counter-balanced to allow its formidable mass to be shifted. To their astonishment, the wall continued to move until it opened into a passageway. They entered the stone shaft behind Dr. Ali and proceeded for six meters through the cramped passage.

The shaft opened into a large, dark room. Dr. Ali took out a small battery-powered lantern and placed it in the center of the room, which came alive with glorious colors and forms.

The room proved to be magnificent in both proportion and content, giving the impression that it was an important ceremonial room. On either side of the vaulted chamber were long stone benches that ran perpendicular to the side walls. The walls were covered in detailed hieroglyphic reliefs, brilliant in color and probably as bright as they were at the moment of execution. Toward the front of the room was a large stone altar that appeared to have been carved out of one massive piece of granite, five meters long, two meters wide and one meter high. The altar was flanked by two imposing sphinx statues seated on large, ornately carved stone blocks covered with hieroglyphs.

Raj exclaimed, "What was this place?" to no one in particular, hearing a peculiar resonance of his voice amplified by the room's natural acoustics. Whatever the purpose of the room, it was awe-inspiring.

Dr. Ali responded, "The hieroglyphs tell an interesting story. You can imagine what we felt when we first entered this chamber: a combination of outright amazement and a deep reverence for the civilization that could create such a monumental place. We immediately got to work and began to photograph and catalog the different *stelae* and hieroglyphics. As this was going on, I took out my note book and began to translate the glyphs, starting on the left and moving around the room in a counter-clockwise direction. By the time I came full circle, a general understanding of the nature of this room and its significance began to emerge. With great excitement, I realized this might be one of the most important discoveries of modern Egyptology. Because, you see, we had entered the inner sanctum–the *Adytum Sanctorius* or Holy of Holies.

"This inner chamber was the sacred ceremonial site for a very special congregation: a place where the initiations of the mystery schools were performed. Once gathered here was an assemblage of the most refined souls of ancient Egypt. These souls were the vanguard of their evolutionary line, the expression of all that was grand and exalted from the flowering of their civilization. Many of the hieroglyphs tell of initiatory rites and ceremonies that were performed fifty centuries ago."

"Dr. Ali, please tell us about these rites?" asked Tamera, politely.

"Yes, of course." Dr. Ali graciously continued, "In this room the sanctified 'ritual Adytum', a series of special tests, were given to selected candidates. The tests were in the form of physical, emotional, mental and spiritual challenges. Each was designed to allow the candidate to demonstrate his mastery of certain ethical and moral qualities and to prove his understanding of the fundamental tenets of spirituality.

"Do the hieroglyphs tell what these skills were?" inquired Raj.

"Yes, they do. This remarkable record is filled with important details revealing the requirements for aspirants qualifying for initiation into the sacred orders. Included were control of the physical body, mobility in various states of consciousness, and dominion over the elements. At the more advanced levels, the aspirant would have to evidence 'special powers' or '*siddhis*', as the Hindus call them. These capabilities might include: mind over matter, or what is now called telekinesis, communication by thought, or telepathy, knowing the history of an object, or psychometry, and various forms of divining the future through the use of oracles. Expression of an inner alignment with the higher Self and spirit guides was also required.

"Pending the outcome of these trials, the fate of the aspirant was determined. The branch of the order he or she would best serve was decided, as was the level of knowledge to be imparted. Only the most capable, wise and compassionate could be trusted with the sacred knowledge. This was knowledge of the true origin of their civilization and of those words of power that would allow them to have dominion over matter. This gave them power in society-power that would keep their civilization evolving on a progressive path throughout the eons.

"This is all represented in the hieroglyphs that surround you," he said, gesturing as he pointed the flashlight around the room. Dr. Ali seemed to be in a state of profound elation as he shared his discovery.

Raj was moved by the depth of meaning presented in the surrounding hieroglyphs and by Dr. Ali's understanding of it all. He must have been an expert reader of the glyphs to interpret their content in such a clear and cogent manner, relating his insight in terms they could all understand. This required an enormous scholarly aptitude that one could only call a "special power" in itself.

"But, that's not all. Take a look at this," Dr. Ali proclaimed, as he focused on an area just behind one of the sphinx statues. He highlighted a series of hieroglyphs that were accentuated by the great Egyptian symbol of Ra, the winged sun disk embraced by the cobra.

"Dr. Ali, please tell us what this says," asked Tamera.

"Yes, this grouping of hieroglyphs immediately drew my attention. In the brief time that I have been going over them, this is the most curious and perhaps the most provocative of the glyphs. First I will give you a literal translation:

STEP PYRAMID

Before Saqqara was, I am. Before the sacred tomb of the first Pharaon was, I am. Having survived the water of the Great Floods, I am. Having preserved the mystery of the horizon, I am. Your womb and seed, I am.

The sun had twice risen where it now sets, and twice set where it now rises, since my beginning.

From my seat, I have watched. I have prepared a place of honor. I have given my symbol, that you may know me. My gift is knowledge. Your future-my legacy.

"Do you understand the implications of this stela?" he questioned. "It goes on to assert that these words are attributed to an ancient stone tablet that was entombed at the foot of the Great Sphinx of Giza. If this is true, and I have absolutely no reason to doubt the authenticity of this stela, the Great Sphinx was present on the Giza plateau long before the Pyramids of Giza were built, and probably long before the beginning of the Pharaonic dynasties. In fact, the line, 'The sun had twice risen where it now sets, and twice set where it now rises, since my beginning,' suggests that the Sphinx was originally created when the processional movement of the earth, on its axis, had completed one and a-half cycles. A single processional cycle takes twenty-six thousand years to complete. This suggests that the Egyptian culture, its language, its hieroglyphs, and probably its science, medicine and architecture as well, were not a direct creation of the Egyptian dynastic civilization, but a legacy. A legacy from a far older civilization, possibly one that came before the great biblical floods. This would suggest a civilization many thousands of years older than the earliest dates we now attribute to the beginning of the Egyptian civilization, or for that matter, human civilization as we have come to know it. Back to a time we had previously considered Neolithic; a time that dates to before the last ice age and the flooding that occurred when the megalithic ice sheets receded."

They were dumbfounded by the implications of Dr. Ali's

insights.

"But, why hasn't a trace of this earlier civilization been found?" asked Raj.

Dr. Ali replied, "We know so little of the pre-dynastic world, especially that of the Nile region. There are no records, no archeological sites, no cross-cultural inferences, just a blank in the annals of time. I can only postulate the existence of a pre-dynastic origin-culture, one that may have migrated from a doomed and disintegrating land, leaving no traces of its civilization. One that had created, through a long period of development, a complex culture replete with art, architecture, agriculture, science and a flourishing language. A language that evolved to articulate the most sublime spiritual understandings.

"This origin-civilization, one that must have pre-dated the great flood, was suggested by Plato to be the fabled Atlantis. As priests, artisans, builders and scribes migrated from their doomed land they brought with them the skills to create the wonders that instantly became Pharaonic Egypt.

"But to utter this word–Atlantis–in Egyptological academic circles is anathema. It is heresy, and the careless mention of the word could ruin one's career.

"Evidence seems to point to the existence of an advanced predecessor civilization. For example, the accepted thinking, with regard to the origin of the Great Sphinx of Giza, is that it was built by the fourth dynasty Pharaoh Chephren, who was thought to be responsible for building the second pyramid of Giza. This theory, we now know, cannot be correct. But even before our discovery, it was a hotly contested subject in many archeological forums. Research has concluded that the face of the Sphinx cannot be that of Chephren, as the facial alignments of known statues of Chephren do not match those of the Great Sphinx. Also, there are geological theories asserting that the weathering patterns of the rock from which the Sphinx was carved were caused by water erosion. And that such patterns would require torrential rains falling over many thousands of years to effect. This kind of scientific approach affirms the antiquity of the Sphinx, because the last time the Sahara had a wet climate, as determined by paleoclimatologists using advanced computer models, was at least ten to fifteen thousand years ago, well before the establishment of the Pharaonic Dynasties.

"In addition, throughout the known history of the Sphinx there is documentary evidence to suggest that it was almost completely buried in sand for the entire dynastic period, except for a brief time during the reign of Thutmosis IV, the Eighteenth Dynasty pharaoh. He had a dream that he would uncover the Sphinx and restore it to its original glory and, in doing so, would ascend to the Pharaonic throne. His dream, of course, came true. Yet, the sands travel quickly in the Sahara, and the Sphinx was known to have been buried up to the neck soon thereafter. It remained covered until recently. It is also interesting to note that sand covering the Sphinx would have protected it from further erosion by wind blown sand, suggesting that any water erosion must have occurred in an earlier epoch. Perhaps the Pharaoh Khaphre was only the first to renovate and clear the sand from the Sphinx, and thus became associated with it. In any case, new evidence suggests that the Sphinx, and the origins of human civilization, are a great deal older than previously considered.

"Of course, Egyptologists, defending their turf, refute the evidence and point out the lack of other monuments that would corroborate this hypothesis. They have their dynastic chronological theories neatly figured out and are reluctant to admit that they might need to revise their academic constructions. They think that humans could only have evolved from primitive tribal hunter/gatherers to our current complex society in a linear fashion, with modern civilization being the most advanced and accomplished, the so-called 'crown of creation'. They discredit the possibility that an ancient, previously unknown, culture might have existed, and that it may have been, in some ways, more advanced than our own. For example, the ability to quarry and dress stones in excess of two hundred tons, as evidenced in the construction of the Sphinx Temple, had surely required advanced techniques that we are today incapable of equaling.

"So, you can see the dilemma that has been created by the renewed attention to the mystery of the Sphinx. I believe that I can now introduce evidence into the argument that will point to the greater antiquity of the Sphinx. At least the debate can continue, and perhaps a search can begin to find evidence of an exalted pre-dynastic culture."

Excited by all he had heard, Raj offered his own theory. "Dr. Ali, perhaps we might consider another answer to this mystery. That is, there are no other monuments of the antediluvians in the Nile Valley. Perhaps the Sphinx was the only monument of its kind, constructed as a marker for a colony or trading outpost of the distant Atlanteans. They simply left their mark by the Nile. Then, at the time of the destruction of their country, the Nile Valley was one of the places to which the remnants of their destroyed civilization fled in order to escape its devastation. Somehow, the Nile Valley was spared from the cataclysm, and so became the cradle of the new civilization. With them, the Atlanteans brought their sciences, writings and religion, and started a new society blessed with the benefits of knowledge accumulated from eons of their own cultural development. Hadn't this also occurred when the Europeans colonized the Americas?"

"Yes, perhaps you're right. An interesting theory, and certainly one that invites further research," Dr. Ali responded. Casually glancing at his watch in the dim light, he reacted, "Ah! Look at the time. I am sorry to say, we must finish our explorations here, as the office is about to close, and there are additional duties that I must perform."

They left the tomb elated by what they had seen, and profoundly grateful for the opportunity to witness an archaeological discovery of such magnitude.

Step Pyramid

Walking back to Dr. Ali's office, they paused to examine the different funerary monuments that could be seen on either side of the road. Both the British and French had archeological missions at Saqqara and were busy excavating certain sections of the complex that showed promise. The British had successfully uncovered the tomb of an advisor to the Pharaoh Tutenkhamun in the necropolis area where many high officials of various pharaohs were entombed. They could see the work areas cordoned-off in the distance.

They reached the office and stopped briefly in the lobby to enjoy another cola from the antiquated dispenser. Dr. Ali said his good-byes and excused himself, running off to his office. Raj wondered what other treasures might lie buried beneath the sands as he gazed at the maps and the profusion of marking pins. He now understood that the pins indicated active digs, sites of potential interest, and areas where excavations were complete. The colored pins numbered in the hundreds, and were only the known working sites. How many sites were unknown, and might reveal evidence of a pre-dynastic link to an antediluvian civilization?

Omar, Raj and Tamera drove back through the desert in deep thought, with hardly a word said between them. Only the soothing sound of a Mozart concerto playing softly on the stereo filled the late afternoon air.

"I need to get back to the hotel," Tamera said. "My boss is probably wondering what happened to me. Perhaps, we can drop you off at the Sphinx for the evening show. It's really something to see. You shouldn't miss it. There is a concession stand there where you can get some refreshments." Tamera was leaning forward from the back seat with her arm affectionately draped over Raj's shoulder. He responded by softly stroking her hand.

"I'd love to go, but it's getting late," Raj said, "Do you think I'll get there with any light left? I'd sure like to do some exploring."

Omar responded, "Oh, there will be some light, but I must tell you the pyramids and the Sphinx at twilight are a rare and wonderful treat. I'm sure the darkness won't inhibit your explorations." He laughed aloud with his voice trailing off in the hum of the engine.

Omar mentioned that he had other business to attend to as well, and they agreed to deliver Raj to the Sphinx.

Chapter 7

THE GUIDE

Raj arrived at the Sphinx as the sun's waning rays sliced an ochre halo through the thick Saharan dust. It was the kiss of Ra, blessing his most noble and enduring monuments. An electric tension bristled in the warm evening air; he had finally arrived at the Great Pyramids.

Beads of sweat ran down his face, small rivulets on an uncharted course, moved only by the occasional swipe of a hand. In the rush to reach the pyramids before nightfall he could only think that his time there would be limited. He paused to get his bearings and ascertain his next step, awed by the immensity of his surroundings.

Raj had come to the pyramids just as the regular light show featuring the Giza ruins was to begin. This evening he was in luck, the show would be in English. Reaching into his pocket, he carefully separated some Egyptian currency from his billfold, paid and entered. The Pyramids of Giza are one of the most enduring destinations of the last five thousand years, a place that draws seekers the way moisture is drawn to the trees that form the greenbelt between the Nile and the vast, empty Sahara.

Before settling in for the show, Raj wandered forward to the temple walls, now and then touching the granite slabs still radiating heat from the day. These great hand-hewn stones formed a maze of passageways, all leading to the unknown. He wanted to follow each path, to see where it would lead, knowing it would be difficult to do so once darkness descended. There was much to explore, but his thoughts were focused on the moment: the heat rising from the fitted-stone causeway, the bare seats beginning to fill with people, the awesome spectacle of the Sphinx scarred from callous human abuse and relentless erosion.

Keeper of Secrets

The spell was snapped when from behind a temple wall, half hidden from view, emerged a small man with short dark hair. Startled, Raj hesitated but allowed him to approach. "Do you wish to explore the temple?" he asked.

Raj nodded in affirmation.

"Then I can show you," he continued, "I am Mohammed and I will be your guide."

His mind raced. Could this be possible? he wondered. Or, perhaps he wants to rob me in some dark, deserted crypt. "But how can we explore the temple at night? Won't it be closed?" Raj inquired, doubting Mohammed.

"I am Mohammed," he said, reaffirming a name that would get a response from most Moslem men in this part of the world, "and the night watchman is my friend."

In that instant the tension dissipated as Raj sensed that there was no danger. Not because it was impossible that Mohammed was a thief, but because of the feeling that it was O.K. to be hustled at that moment; an opportunity awaited and perhaps an adventure. Besides, Mohammed had invoked a higher authority: "The Night Watchman".

They made a plan. After the show, Raj would return to the same spot, where Mohammed would be waiting. Then the adventure would begin. Raj was thrilled with the prospect of a moonlit evening among the ancient ruins, monumental edifices baked by a million days of sun, and still echoing with voices resounding through the millennia.

He wandered back to the amphitheater and slowly settled into a rigid plastic seat, in one of four rows laid out on a hard-packed dusty floor. There was no bad seat in the house, he mused, as the sky turned indigo against the barely perceptible monuments.

Opening a large bottle of cool Cairo ale delivered by a vendor carrying an enormous metal case strapped over his shoulder, he drank deeply, almost inhaling the piquant brew. A stream of energy surged up his spine and sent a slight shiver coursing through his body. Its residual voltage left his fingertips buzzing. The signs of ancient spirits swirling in the vicinity, he thought. The night breeze grazed his skin like fine silk pulled slowly but deliberately across his bare arms. Perhaps it was a subtle ethereal veil of an other-worldly apparition trailing against him.

With heightened awareness and a sense of deep relaxation, he was ready to take in the evening's presentation. The lights came up revealing the Sphinx in crimson glory, the show had begun.

It seemed as though hours had passed as the pageant of pharaonic history was told in a familiar, accessible way. Yet Raj was restless as the sky had already turned a deep black, in contrast to the light show which gave motion and life to the monuments. He was there but not really listening. His mind was absorbed in the events of the day and explorations yet to begin. He felt that he was being compelled by an unknown, unseen force that was guiding his actions. Time seemed compressed, as if each moment were filled to overflowing.

The flood lights dimmed as the show ended. The house lights came up and the crowd began to depart. He hesitated for a moment and considered whether or not to meet Mohammed. After all, he was quite tired and the pyramids weren't going anywhere. There was always tomorrow and the light of day. However, it seemed that he was being driven by forces greater than fear, doubt and fatigue. A sense of destiny and a lust for experience prevailed. He walked slowly and deliberately down the causeway toward the massive stone edifice that formed the entrance to the temple. He waited, wondering whether Mohammed would show.

The amphitheater had closed, leaving him alone, dwarfed by the towering, silent megaliths. He paced beside the temple walls admiring the smooth stone surface, now and then feeling its texture with a casual outstretched hand. He could hear the distant sound of voices and laughter as small groups began to congregate at the base of the Great Pyramid–a local custom, probably going back to the time when they were first constructed.

He turned and was startled by the appearance of a figure who seemed to emerge from the shadows. It was Mohammed: the guide had arrived.

"Did you enjoy the show?" he asked, with enthusiasm.

"Yes, it was fine," Raj replied. "Quite an experience."

"You know, in pharaonic times we were a great people. We built these monuments and they have lasted, even until today. The pharaon had the great knowledge, and we keep their memory," he said, expressing a deep reverence for his surroundings. "We must go now, if you want to explore the tombs." He continued nervously, "Are you ready to go?"

"Sure, but what do you want for being my guide? How much? *Baksheesh*?" Raj asked, as he motioned with his thumb and forefingers, rubbing them together in the time-honored fashion indicating money.

"I am Mohammed and I am your friend. I will take care of you now and you can take care of me later. For now, I ask nothing."

Since Raj wanted to begin the adventure, he nodded in agreement and followed him into the darkness.

With only a small flashlight between them, they made their way into the labyrinth that surrounded the outer approaches to the Sphinx. At first they entered a small mastabah which dead-ended quickly and was notable only for the immense granite slabs comprising its ceiling. It sparkled as the flashlight's beam swept across it. Mohammed noted this effect with some glee, as if he were looking at the laser light show of a modern planetarium.

Raj's interest in this line of exploration faded quickly and he became impatient. Visiting the old tombs at night seemed incredible at the onset, but these tombs had long ago been stripped of anything of real interest. They were stone shells whose life's blood had drained away into the porous desert sand. Mohammed seemed to know the whereabouts of dozens of small funerary rooms and took delight in walking into each one of them. Some were gated, perhaps concealing secret pathways to underground tunnels said to honeycomb the area. More likely, Raj thought, the gates were there to cover up the sorry state of the graves. They had been looted and re-looted by each successive generation that made these tombs a place of commerce and sustenance.

Raj wanted something more meaningful. Finally, he asked Mohammed, "Can we get closer to the pyramids and perhaps climb one?"

"You must know this is forbidden," Mohammed retorted sternly, though his hard demeanor seemed to fade quickly.

Raj, however, sensed that he could be accommodated in some way.

"But maybe I can help you," continued Mohammed. "It would be a special favor. We can go to the third pyramid–Mekyrnos, but we must walk there and it is a long walk on the soft sand. Are you sure you want to go?"

This was exactly what Raj was looking for, so he eagerly agreed. They set off from the tombs and began to walk to the south and west toward Mykernos. The moon was full, its brightness illuminating the landscape with a pale blue-white iridescence, casting elongated shadows and creating a dance of perceptible and barely perceptible forms. Ahead of them they could see some movement. Mohammed ran to find out what it was, quickly returning with his report.

"The men ahead are the camel drivers who serve the tourists during the day. I asked them if they would be willing to take us to Mekyrnos. Do you want to ride?"

Raj nodded in agreement and asked, "What will they want to take us there?"

"These are my friends," Mohammed answered, "and for me they offer a special price. They only ask twenty Egyptian pounds. It is a very good price, extra special, and I offer this to you because you are my friend. You must pay me now and I will give them the money."

Raj was weary, and the thought of negotiating seemed trying, so he agreed to the price. "Tell the camelmen that I'll pay them half now and half when we arrive." As this seemed reasonable, Mohammed agreed.

The camel drivers came over with their beasts, which knelt in the sand with a series of commands and whistles accompanied by vigorous prodding. Raj boarded the largest camel, named Ramses I, which was lavishly outfitted with Bedouin ceremonial camel-wear. Mohammed mounted Ramses II, its smaller cousin, also festooned with the latest in colorful dromedary accessories. With a few brief words of encouragement, the camels stood up, made a grunting snort, and surged forward toward the third pyramid with a loping gait. The moon was low in the desolate Saharan night as they rode to Mekyrnos or, as the ancient Egyptians knew it to be, the Pyramid of the Pharaoh Menkaure.

The breeze created by the camel's strut through the still night air was a welcome relief from the heat of the day. The camels seemed to glide in a wave-like motion that reminded Raj of the gentle Hawaiian surf off Maui's western coast. The only sound was the thumping of hooves and the camels' snorting, rhythmic breaths. The camels were prodded often by their drivers, and with each poke they responded with renewed vigor in their stride. Time passed quickly. The journey, which might have taken a half hour by foot, lasted only ten minutes.

They reached the base of Menkaure, and with a few select words from the drivers, the camels knelt down on their front legs, and then their hind, causing a whiplash-like movement on the way down. The drivers were paid the balance of ten pounds, plus a baksheesh of five, and they quickly disappeared into the night.

The Pyramid of Menkaure, though the smallest of the three Great Pyramids, has a formidable presence. Its mass and height project a stunning majesty, especially when lit up by ten thousand watts of high-intensity flood lamps. Raj noticed the seeming disarray of the huge stone blocks that form the pyramid. It was different from Cheops and Chephren, which were more perfect even in their decay. He wandered up to the first tier of stones and touched the rough-hewn, jagged granite. His heart began to race as he contemplated the ascent. Turning to Mohammed, he indicated that he was ready to climb, signaling with an upward hand gesture.

"I'm heading up," Raj said, not waiting for permission, as he pulled himself up the first tier of stones. That wasn't bad, he thought. Each tier was waist-high, and required him to thrust-lift his own weight, like vaulting a fence. He settled into a rhythm, first pulling himself up with his arms and then pushing with his legs as he scrambled to the next tier. After scaling several tiers, his heart was pounding and he realized it wasn't going to be an easy climb. But with determination he continued on, pausing every nine or ten tiers to catch his breath.

Mohammed was behind Raj, struggling to maintain his own pace, obviously out of shape. After what seemed like an eternity, Raj began to wonder when the top of the pyramid would appear. Looking up, he realized that he was only half-way there, but his excitement was enough to propel him to the top. Finally, he mounted the stone blocks at the top of the pyramid, straining every ounce of muscle in his body.

The top was a large area with a number of stone blocks strewn about. Perhaps at some point in the distant past, the apex was finished in polished limestone and terminated in an exact point capped in pure gold. But now it was only a ruin with the stones at the top positioned somewhat indiscriminately. There was one stone, however, that was the highest, and upon that stone Raj triumphantly stood to witness a bizarre spectacle. He was surrounded by hundreds of bats out for their evening feed. They were flying in haphazard flight paths, like moths around a flame. This unnerving sight was highlighted by an unusual inverse pyramid of light projected upon the dusty sky by the large flood lamps used to illuminate the pyramid. Around this vortex of light the thumping flutter of thousands of bat wings could be heard. Raj stood up in this cacophony of flying forms for about thirty seconds. He immediately sat down with his back against the uppermost stone. Mohammed joined him there, huffing and wheezing as he reached the top.

"Jesus! Mohammed, you didn't tell me there were bats up here!" he exclaimed.

"Oh, yes, Mr. Raj, there are bats," was Mohammed's response, barely articulated in his breathless condition.

They sat at the top of the pyramid for about an hour, enjoying the cool evening breezes from the desert plain. The stones, however, were still warm, radiating heat accumulated from a day in the blistering sun. Raj was amazed at being there, and was especially fascinated by the view of Cheops and Chephren from his elevated vantage point. The top of Menkaure rose two hundred and fifteen feet above the Giza plateau, about half way up the other pyramids. As he bathed in the energy fields emanating from the sacred geometry of the pyramid, he looked down and noticed the Sphinx sitting in its illuminated splendor.

"Mohammed," he inquired, "can we go down and visit the Sphinx?"

"Oh yes, Mr. Raj, this we can do. I will take you there."

"Let's go," proclaimed Raj, as he got up and, with renewed vitality, began bounding down the tiered stones, jumping from level to level like a mountain goat. Mohammed was in close pursuit, and before long they were down. Raj was invigorated by the quick descent, but his legs ached and felt like rubber.

They continued by foot to the Sphinx. As they approached, they could see a barbed-wire fence surrounding the monument, making it impossible to get close. The only way to approach the torso was through a guarded, gated entryway. The Sphinx was undergoing repairs and was off limits to everyone but the authorized stone masons and officials from the Egyptian Antiquities Organization.

The Sphinx had undergone numerous restorations during its long history, commencing in recorded time with the Pharaoh Chephren. Although generally credited with its original construc-

The Guide

tion, he was probably responsible only for its restoration. Evidence suggests he might even have carved the hind section out of the surrounding rock.

Another major Sphinx improvement project is credited to the Eighteenth Dynasty Pharaoh Thutmosis IV, who, legend says, was visited by the Sphinx in a dream when he was a young prince and was told that he would ascend to the throne if he uncovered and restored the Sphinx to its former glory. Until Thutmosis IV, the Sphinx had been buried up to the neck in sand for over a thousand years (since the time of Chephren). Eventually, he completed the restoration and fulfilled the prophesy by ascending the pharaonic throne. A stela was erected and positioned between the paws of the Sphinx to commemorate the fulfillment of his dream.

Raj wanted to touch the Sphinx but it was fenced off in an unauthorized area. He asked Mohammed plaintively, "Can you get me to the base of the Sphinx?"

"I will talk to the gatekeeper. He is my friend. I'll see what I can do."

They proceeded rather stealthily past the old temple walls toward the official viewing area. It was as if they were conducting a commando raid, because Mohammed deemed it necessary to crouch down and move carefully in the shadows, lest they be seen. When they reached the gate, Mohammed went ahead to talk with the guard. Within a few moments he reappeared.

"The guard is my friend, and says he can let us in, but you need to give him baksheesh."

"How much?" inquired Raj, not particularly surprised.

"Ten pounds."

"All right," Raj responded, as he handed ten Egyptian pounds to Mohammed. Ten pounds! He might have been outraged, but to touch the Sphinx was a bargain at any price. He was happy to pay. They entered through the gate and walked to the Sphinx, moving quickly in the shadows to avoid the authorities. Within moments they were between the paws of the Sphinx, looking directly up at its enormous head which was pock-marked from artillery fire that blew off its nose two hundred years earlier (an unfortunate act attributed to the Mameluks: zealous eighteenth century Turkish rulers).

It was an awesome sight and Raj's heart was pounding. He could feel the power of the place, the hairs on the nape of his neck bristling. He could almost hear the ancient footsteps of pharaonic priests in procession, leading young neophytes into a hidden temple accessed through the extended paws of the Sphinx. Raj considered its long existence and the countless souls whose veneration made the site holy. He could only marvel at a monument that could survive as long as it had. The longevity and presence of the Sphinx had given it a respect that surpassed all other man-made monuments. Seeking to immortalize the moment, he took his camera out of his shoulder bag and snapped a classic shot–straight up at the Sphinx's jutting jaw.

He made his way around the side of the Sphinx to examine the repair work being conducted to create a smooth surface around its lower flanks. The new stone cover protected the original crumbling stones from the accelerated decay caused by the modern stresses of air pollution and acid rain. Small stone blocks, expertly crafted, were fitted into place and mortared with precision and care. Above the area of recent work were the ancient stones of the old statue showing the effects of extensive erosion.

The front of the Sphinx exhibited erosion scars that were three to four feet deep. This kind of wear is consistent with long-term water erosion and is also reflected in the stone walls excavated around the Sphinx and in the giant stone blocks of the Sphinx Temple. Geological weathering of this sort requires extensive rains falling over many thousands of years. Since the Sphinx was covered with sand for most of the last four to five thousand years, this weathering must have occurred prior to the early dynastic period, an indication of its extreme age. Evidence points to a chronological age of ten to fifteen thousand years, pre-dating the dynasties of pharaonic Egypt by several thousand years. This still did not answer the critical question: who built the Sphinx and why? The mystery remained.

With impatience Mohammed suggested, "We should be going now. It's dangerous for us to stay here too long. We might be found by the police, and this we do not want. Please, Mr. Raj, let's go."

"O.K., where to?" responded Raj, hoping to linger at the feet of the Sphinx a little longer.

"It is time to visit my friend–the Night Watchman."

Keeper of Secrets

Chapter 8

THE NIGHT WATCHMAN

Raj and Mohammed left the Sphinx and walked toward a nearby plateau, past abandoned tombs and ancient stone columns. The moonlight cast long, uneven shadows from the surrounding ruins. They followed the path as it wound up and around the lower tombs to a flattened hill with a commanding view of the pyramids. At the top of the rise was a squat one-story mud hut with a wooden door and a single barred window.

The late evening air had become exceptionally clear without the usual dusty Saharan pall. The stars seemed animated by ripples of heat rising off the pyramids. Their outline was silhouetted by a cobalt blue glow radiating from the far western sky such as one can see on late summer evenings. In front of the hut was an open fire pit surrounded by irregular chunks of limestone. A blazing fire was burning. The hut appeared to undulate through the pattern of the flames which were fueled from the combustion of broken crates and a never-ending supply of camel dung.

Mohammed approached the hut and knocked while Raj waited patiently by the fire. A large man appeared at the door. He spoke briefly to Mohammed and disappeared into the hut.

"We're in luck," Mohammed related, returning to Raj, "the Night Watchman will see us. He is preparing tea and said we should make ourselves at home."

Raj wondered what that could possibly mean, as he found a flat rock close to the fire and sat down.

The Night Watchman emerged carrying a tray with glasses and a porcelain pot of hot tea. He walked slowly toward the fire, carefully balancing the tray on one hand while using his other hand as a counter-balance. He placed the tray on a large flat-hewn stone and pulled up an old wooden chair. He was silent as he sat pouring the tea into small clear glasses, carefully aiming the spout to avoid spilling the steaming liquid. He passed around the glasses, sipping casually from his own. Breaking the silence he addressed his guests. "I have been the night watchman of the Pyramids of Giza for the past nineteen years. Night after night I sit through the still, calm hours of the early morning. This is a special time of serene and tranquil energy on the Giza Plateau. Rarely is this serenity broken until dawn, when the surrounding neighborhoods come to life and I can go home and rest." He spoke calmly in a deep raspy voice with a thick Arabic accent.

Raj nodded in silent testimony as he slowly sipped the soothing tea, gazing upon the incredible scene that stretched out before him. This is a man, he thought, who has spent many years sitting in quiet meditation, year after year, at the foot of these magnificent monuments. It must have had some effect on him.

Then out of the blue and with an unexpected sense of urgency, Raj turned to Mohammed and asked, "Do you have something for me?" He didn't really know why he said this, it just dropped into his mind and came out of his mouth as if deliberate and well-thought-out.

Mohammed rose up and exclaimed, "Yes I do! I will go and get it." Without another word he disappeared into the night.

With Mohammed gone, the Night Watchman looked intently into Raj's eyes and immediately declared, "I have been waiting for you." His voice and demeanor had shifted remarkably, with a complete transformation of elocution and accent.

"Really?" Raj responded, startled by the metamorphosis, "How did you know I was coming?"

"I know many things," he answered. "I know who you are, and why you have come. I know where you have been and where you are going."

Raj was mystified by this pronouncement and somewhat taken aback. After all, he wasn't even entirely sure why he was there.

How could the Night Watchman know? Raj thought he could have just as easily gone back to the hotel for a nights sleep instead.

"But you didn't," replied the Night Watchman, seemingly responding to Raj's innermost thoughts.

That got Raj's attention. "Who are you?" he asked. He realized that someone who could say that, who could know his past and his future, read his thoughts and sense his emotions, would be someone quite extraordinary, someone endowed with a higher level of insight or–a profound mystical power.

"Suffice it to say that I am more than I appear to be. Although the position of the Night Watchman is not an exalted post, I have been chosen to watch over the pyramids and their secrets. This I do while others are asleep. It is a sacred trust, and I take my responsibilities very seriously."

"I'm sure that you do, but that still doesn't explain how you come to know me, or why you were expecting me."

"How I come to know you is not important, that I do is," he answered. "There are times when you must face your destiny, because it will unfold before you whether you accept it or not. Cooperate in awareness or resist and be carried off in a whirlwind. Which do you choose?" The Night Watchman became pensive, and his voice took on a stern quality, as he continued, "There is much we do not understand about life, but we keep searching for answers. We look for signs and indications that can lead us forward and help us to reach our goals. But many are uncertain of their destiny or the part in life they must play. They turn away from the truths that call out to them, losing themselves in the shallow quest for material accumulations. Or they are consumed in the struggle for survival. Often they simply forget the call of their inner life and, after a time, the voice within becomes stilled, withering away.

"But you must understand, they are never abandoned by their inner guides, no matter how disinterested or confused they may become. As long as they haven't completely severed the sacred thread of contact, by some savage act, there is hope. There are messages, sign posts, and indications along the way that are divinely sent. They are placed on the road of life for the benefit of the soul. But they must be invoked by intense striving."

The Night Watchman's voice was filled with emotion as he continued, "When you feel in your heart that you are part of a greater awareness, know that you are, because you are being touched by the inner guide–the source of inspiration and the connection to the greater family of souls. When you feel there is more to life than the seemingly endless cycles of mundane experience, know that there is, and that awareness of a greater destiny is an important step on the Path. When you sense that there are others who are searching like you, know that there are, and that they thirst for the experience of knowledge and truth. Understand that there are others who have searched for truth before you, and know that a sacred trust compels each soul to sacrifice on the way in order to shed light on the path of those who follow. This is the Great Service to which all servers of light dedicate their lives. You are never alone in your quest, for there is help for all those who try, with their hearts and minds, to reach beyond the self–to touch the light. And, there is always help for those who wish to preserve and uphold the truth.

"I come to know you, because your striving has brought you to Our attention. You have caused a spiritual response by your thoughts and actions, especially those consecrated to love, light and truth. I know your heart and I know your mind, because you have caused them to emanate a sacred radiance.

"As each day passes, the great story of life is unfolding, inscribed with the destiny of humanity in which we all play a part. Everyone has a story to tell, everyone is a part of the great mosaic, an essential thread in the tapestry of life. We must, however, be tested and tried, our experience gained and our knowledge and wisdom earned. The field of experience we call life is really a school where our souls learn to work in substance and matter. In this way, we come to learn of our destined roles as co-creators with God, evolving in light unto the sacred threshold of Ra.

"You will now receive a great understanding, one which is vitally important to all who strive with compassion and hope for the future."

The Night Watchman appeared to swoon as he lapsed into a state of deep meditation. Raj knew he needed to remain perfectly still. Slowly, the Night Watchman regained his equilibrium and began a new discourse, as if the voltage in his being had suddenly increased.

"To encourage the souls of humanity to strive to perfection," he began, "the Great Ones have sent out their emissaries. They are the 'Keepers of Secrets,' of truth, knowledge and wisdom. Their numbers are small, but they have watchful eyes and can see into the depths of one's being. They see and know with the mind's eye through 'straight knowledge' (the direct contact with essential beingness), and can know your heart and your thoughts, both past and present. With total love and compassion, they recognize that within you which is divine and pure. And they accept that in you which needs refinement, knowing that the path toward light is a long and arduous one. It is because of their infinite compassion, patience and solemn dedication that the flame of truth has never been extinguished, and the path of light has always remained open.

"I am an emissary from those who work for the light, the servants of the whole–the ancient Brotherhood of Ra. Our work has gone on uninterrupted through all times and in all places. There has never been a time when humankind has been without this guidance.

"It is an honor to carry out a sacred mission and an honor to be chosen. For few are prepared to undertake a such a task, and few are willing to make the sacrifice needed to become prepared. Our lives are dedicated to assisting the souls of humankind in the unfoldment of their spirit consciousness.

"The Brotherhood of Ra are guardians of the plan for safekeeping knowledge. It is our task to preserve the wisdom of the ages. In the long history of the earth there has never been a time, such as now, where a total immersion into material existence has dominated human consciousness. However, throughout this crucial period, the living light has been preserved to guide our development, ensuring that every soul can walk the path of Light.

"We are now at a time in human history where the fate of humankind will be decided. The dates have arrived, and the time for waiting is finished. All is in play, and what I have been sent to do, I must do. You have arrived, by way of a path that you yourself have created, and now you must prepare for the undertaking that is your duty to fulfill.

"What I must reveal to you is an understanding of the great origins passed down through the ages. We have come to the days foretold by the ancestors when the 'Opening of the Way' will be revealed. The Great Ancient of Days, the Omniscient Ra, in whom we live, move and have our being, has foreseen the long passage through time, and has prepared the way for a safe transition."

Raj was entranced by the oratory of the Night Watchman. Despite his outer appearance, the Night Watchman was a man of refinement whose masterful speech belied his simple dress and demeanor. He appeared ancient and abounding with wisdom, but he also had a simple child-like nature.

Raj sensed a moment of destiny unfolding before him. He composed himself and entered a receptive, hypnotic state, so that he could absorb as much as possible. He took several deep cleansing breaths in order to focus his attention, then exhaled and waited for the Night Watchman's story to unfold.

Chapter 9

ORIGINS

The Night Watchman slowly rose from his creaking old chair in a single, strained motion. His formidable gelabia, billowing in an errant breeze, hid the details of his movements. He trudged over to a pile of broken crates that looked as if they had been struck with a sledge hammer. Carefully selecting an armful of debris, he made his way to the fire and threw two pieces on the glowing coals, along with a shovel-full of camel dung from a nearby dung heap. The fire responded immediately, consuming the dry splinters, while the dung smoldered and infused the air with its acrid stench.

This simple activity left the Night Watchman breathing hard as he eased himself back into his chair. He pensively watched the fire whose intensifying inferno produced a series of sky-licking flames. Casually reaching over to the delicate china tea pot, he poured another round of tea.

Raj took the opportunity to find a place on the far side of the mud hut to relieve himself, scanning the dim outline of the pyramids that dominated the horizon. He returned to his place by the fire, a flat block of eroded limestone. It was ancient and impregnated with human history, a monument to the memories of the past.

Most temple stones in ancient Egypt had been used and reused in the building of new structures that periodically replaced outworn sites of worship. This was a tradition that even the mediaeval Arabs continued as they built their mosques from the casing stones of ancient monuments. They used these abandoned structures for convenient quarry material. The Egyptian priests of old made the recycling of sacred stones a deliberate practice and understood their deep significance. The magnetic powers of the old stones were used to seed the newer temples with their sanctified energy. These ancient blocks of limestone and granite were infused with the energy of solemn veneration from ritual worship performed over eons. When they found an especially potent stone, like a phallus taken from a pharaonic image, they would re-install the stone at a new temple in a specially carved frieze, usually between the legs of the image of the latest pharaoh as a deliberate display of potency, virility and sovereignty. To be used again and again, was the fate of many of the temple stones–their antiquity beyond casual calculation, their origins obscured in the remote past. Yet they might also be used as a seat by an open fire, a monumental fragment now employed in the simple service of life.

The Night Watchman settled into his seat, soothing his dry throat by steadily sipping tea. His appearance changed from moment to moment as he shifted his position, allowing each square centimeter of his mass to react fully with gravity and the resistance of his wooden, straight-backed chair. He became comfortable, and in a steady but impassioned tone he began to tell his tale.

"The story I must tell is one of the great stories of the ages. It is a story of the foresight of the Brotherhood of Ra and its love for the generations yet to be born. It is a story of the brave souls facing the dark ages to come and of the courage required to carry out a sacred mission."

The Night Watchman looked off into the distance and continued, "I will tell you of a time when the mighty pharaon and his people had reached the height of their remarkable civilization. It was during the Fourth Dynasty reign of the beneficent Pharaoh Khufu, when their greatest achievement was about to be realized–the completion of the Great Pyramid.

"To commemorate the achievement an inauguration ceremony was held of a grandeur the world had never before witnessed. The ceremony was the final act of consecration, when the pyramid was capped in pure gleaming gold, and a series of sacred rituals were performed to infuse the structure with a vital presence. The pyramid was established as a beacon of light, as an altar to Ra and as the inner sanctum for the initiation of the soul.

"By the light of day, the polished gilded cap of the Great Pyramid radiated a sun-like quality which could be seen for miles. It was as if the sun had been brought to earth, its rays bathing the surrounding valley in an amber hue, imbuing everything with a patina of honeyed radiance. It was the emanation of Ra.

"The pyramid's perfect alignment with the earth endowed it with unique celestial observational capabilities. The massive structure was large enough to be seen from above revealing an understanding of cosmic relationships, which were infused into the design. The Great Pyramid was truly an outpost of the gods.

"The pyramid's geodetic alignment linked it with the stars through light, sacred geometry and spiritual intent. It was used in this way during the consecration ceremony. The rite was precisely timed to occur at the exact moment of the helical or dawn rising of the constellation of Orion. It was at this time that the light of the star Zeta Orionis, found in Orion's belt, and the star Sirius aligned with the inner shafts of the Great Pyramid. The shafts were constructed to channel the light of these stars to the inner sanctums of the King's and Queen's Chambers. These channels of light were pathways for the spirit, or *Aakhu*, of the pharaoh to commune with the divine origins, renewing its cycle of birth and resurrection. It was through this contact that the pharaoh sought to attain immortality.

"The pharaohs were considered the symbols of human perfection and so were chosen to commune with the exalted stellar deities. The star Sirius was recognized as Isis, the Great Mother of Regeneration and Goddess of Fertility. The pharaoh assumed the role of Osiris, paramour of Isis, whose divine seed caused life to stir in Isis. He enacted this in a divine play, paying homage to Isis. It was She who was honored as the mother of Ra. Sirius, being the astronomical and spiritual center of our Sun, is the central star around which our sun orbits in the course of its cycle of being.

Keeper of Secrets

This relationship was understood by the ancients, who recognized Sirius as the sacred star of our origins."

The Night Watchman paused and raised his arm in a sudden sweeping movement toward the sky. There, high above the Giza Plateau, a shooting star arched across the sky moving from east to west, its fiery tail luminescing in a smoking, effusive trail. Its direction was suggestive of the path of the passing pharaon, east to west, to the land of death, rebirth and regeneration. It was a sign affirming the spiritual destiny unfolding before them.

The Night Watchman sat in thought, contemplating the heavenly sign, and then continued, "In the course of time, three Pyramids towered over Giza, called by the ancients Rostau. They formed the Horizon of Rostau, which was considered a gateway to the stars with direct access to heaven. When seen from above, the pyramids were laid out in perfect accord and symmetry, mirroring the three central stars that form the belt of the constellation Orion. They were positioned to reflect the celestial locations of Orion's belt stars in relation to the languid Nile, whose north flowing path closely resembled the course of the stellar Milky Way. In fact, the positioning reflected the heavens as they appeared in the distant past, with the stellar alignments pointing to a precise moment.

"It was a moment when the founders of ancient Egypt, intending to convey a message to future generations, established the Great Pyramid. They instructed their architects to create a monument that would last through the millennia. This required a vision that would span many generations, and when completed would not only create an image on earth of what they observed in the heavens, but would fix in stone knowledge about the earth's movements at a point in earth's history between epochal cataclysms, marking the location of true north and, transmitting, in a subtle code, a special knowledge."

"What was this knowledge?" Raj asked.

"The knowledge embodied in the Great Pyramid revealed information about the origins of human consciousness and the role the stars play in the development of life. You see, there is a chain of concordant consciousness that links sentient beings together. Consciousness emanates from the stars themselves and is understood to exist throughout the universe. The ancients looked to the stars for the source of both their spiritual and their material beginnings.

"And wisely so, for we now know that elements integral to the formation of complex life can only be formed in the heat of stellar explosions. The dust left over from these explosions coalesces in the primordial clouds of interstellar space to become new stars and planets, such as our Sun and Earth. This dust includes heavier elements which are essential to life, such as carbon and iron, and is the source of some of the critical raw materials needed for the inception of life. We are all made of 'star dust' and owe our existence to the great stellar forms that lived and died billions of years ago."

The Night Watchman stopped his narrative, momentarily pausing to sip his neglected cup of tea. It was a balm to his throat, made raspy by his inspired soliloquy. Breathing deeply he continued with renewed fervor.

"The Mother Star, Isis/Sirius, is the source of the souls who populate our planet. Our souls are all star-born, and our destiny is to return to the stars. A great host of souls traveled with the solar deity, Ra, when the journey was made from Sirius to inspirit our star system. Those souls, called the Aakhu by the ancient priests, eventually incarnated on earth, where conditions for human existence were established."

"If we are related to the stars, could this be the basis for astrology?"

"Yes. In fact, your so-called astrology is what the Brotherhood calls 'the Science of the Luminaries'. It defines the relationships and affinities that exist between the stars and their progeny. We are the offspring of the stars and are impacted by the complex interrelationships of the luminaries through their emanations.

Keeper of Secrets

Each celestial life projects through light, gravity, and a subtle, spiritual force the ancients called 'aka', its essence, into the firmament. These strings of force weave a cosmic net, and this net is the womb of the worlds. Your western scientists have talked of the 'string theory' and how it underpins the universe; this is a similar concept. It forms the basis of the awesome associations of stars we call galaxies which whirl through the infinity of space in numbers that are inconceivable to the human mind. A special place in the cosmic net is provided to each new star, within which lines of relationship are created between all existing stars. These emanations are composed of threads of aka which bind the celestial universe. This substance is integral to life, and so, we are bound to the influences of all celestial bodies, especially our own Sun.

"It is this matrix of stellar and planetary relationships that is cast as our natal or birth horoscope. It defines the place of the luminaries as they were at the moment of our birth, and the inflection of their qualities upon our new lives. However, this is just a blueprint, a framework, as it were, and every person is free to develop as they choose. We must, however, realize how strongly we are influenced by the power of the stars and planets."

"Do Sirius and Orion play an important role in our world?" Raj wondered out loud.

"Stars closest to each other in distance and movement have relationships with very strong affinities. Such is the case with Sirius and the Orion stars. These stellar associations are hierarchically grouped into luminous relationships that form the basis of galactic life. Our Milky Way is such a life. Our Sun is only one of billions of stars that form our galaxy, and there are countless billions of galaxies. Such is the glorious and infinite nature of the Universe.

"This great reverence for the star Sirius by the ancients was a recognition of the divine origins of human consciousness. Sirius was considered to be the living incarnation of the Goddess Isis, the divine Mother, in whose womb all life was created. Veneration of the Holy Mother was a fundamental principle of the Brotherhood of Ra, who practiced their loving devotion as an essential covenant in their spiritual life. The paths to higher understanding and wisdom opened through the portals of Isis. Ra could not be approached without initiation into the Temple of Isis, for to serve Isis was to serve the regeneration of all life."

At that moment a rustle could be heard from below the rise of the hill, accompanied by the sound of approaching footsteps. The Night Watchman fell silent, wary to speak aloud before an unidentified stranger. Emerging from the shadows was an out-of-breath Mohammed. Quietly, he sat down beside Raj.

The Night Watchman excused himself, and got up from his chair. He made his way to the hut, tea pot in hand.

"Nice of you to return," Raj observed.

"Yes, *Hamdul El Lah*, and I have something very special, very beautiful. It is a gift for you." He reached into his jacket and pulled out a small, metal statuette. It had the green patina of oxidized copper and a feeling of antiquity that made Raj's heart race. It was the Goddess Isis, seated with the child Horus suckling at Her breast. Upon Her head was the symbol of Ra, the sun disk framed in the *Uraeus* of eternal life. Raj considered its age, but didn't ask, knowing that it could easily be a relatively new piece, made to look old. He was more impressed by the symbology of the gesture. Its appearance could not have been more appropriate, a wonderful synchronicity and an affirmation of the moment.

"This is a beautiful gift," Raj said in admiration. "How can I repay you?"

"No pay," replied Mohammed, "this is meant for you, it is a gift."

The Night Watchman returned from his hut with his tray in hand upon which his porcelain pot steamed freely. He sat down and poured a stream of tea from the pot, embellishing his actions by raising the pot as he poured. A thin stream of amber-colored tea sparkled as it fell through the air, reflecting random flashes of flame from the ebbing fire.

Raj responded again to Mohammed with sincere gratitude. "Shukran my friend, I will cherish this for life. I am a great lover of the Mother of the World and believe Her veneration is essential for the survival of our planet. How did you know this was for me? After all, I didn't say what I was asking for."

Mohammed said nothing to this inquiry. However, one look in the direction of the Night Watchman told Raj who was behind the offering. He caught a subtle glint from the Night Watchman's eye. Mohammed was merely the messenger and had been under the suggestion of his hypnotic gaze, a power which played seriously upon his own thinking.

"Mohammed," the Watchman said, with a commanding inflection, "please have a seat by the fire and join us. I see that you have presented our guest with a momento of his night by the pyramids. The Holy Mother Isis is a fitting symbol, for we all must serve the Great Mother who gives us life and nourishes us. She is Mother Nature Herself and, without Her, life would not exist."

Mohammed was instructed to tend the fire and keep it even, so a consistent, radiant warmth could be felt. He undertook the job with a particular zeal, poking and arranging the fire often. Small piles of charred wood collapsed into the remaining coals as fresh wood burst into flames, animating their facial expressions.

The Night Watchman continued, "The pharaohs were the Sons of Isis," he said. "It was She that birthed them and She who nurtured and suckled them. They were the sons of the star-born deities and this gave them their divine authority to rule. Each dying pharaoh became an Osiris because, through Osiris, immortality could be achieved. As each passing pharaoh made this transition, his heir became Horus, son of Osiris and Isis. In this way the divine right of ascension to the pharaonic throne was preserved and sanctified.

"The pharaohs themselves worshipped at the altar of Isis, for She was the Goddess of the mysteries and of insight into the

Origins

ancient wisdom that led to the path of immortality. In the earliest times, She was known as Au Sept, a name that means ancient of ancients, and Her star, Sirius, appeared on the horizon on the longest day, a sign of the triumph of light. This time also coincided with the yearly Nile flood which brought fertility to the land, another compassionate act of nourishment that lent glory to Her name. She was known as the Mother of All Life and as the Restorer of Life. The very power of the pharaoh was Her gift, as Isis was considered to be the Throne of Egypt. It has been written in the most ancient texts: 'In the beginning there was Isis, Oldest of the Old. She was the Goddess from Whom all becoming arose.' All life progressed in the primordial past through Isis, and unto Her exalted presence we shall all proceed as we make our way toward the great homecoming of light, in our distant future."

The stars played clock in the night sky, advancing their rotational sweep against the megalithic tops of Khufu, Khaphre and Menkaure. As it has always been, the sky was resplendent with the shining presence of thousands of stars whose light is their own life's radiance cast into the firmament. Only our own wobbly spinning globe could create the grand illusion of a procession of luminaries dancing across the sky. Only the creative imaginations of our ancestors could assign the random patterns of stars their symbolic identities. Only from our small planet with its unique point of view could the stars appear as they had to the ancients, who assigned them with imagery and meaning.

Raj had noted the apparent movement of the constellations in the night sky and, despite the teaching revealed to him, knew the evening was passing. He felt exhausted and he was about to fall off his rock when the Night Watchman motioned to Mohammed to catch their dozing guest before he hit the ground.

Startled his body spasmed as he regained his balance. His eyes were opened from the adrenaline-driven surge. "Oh, I'm sorry. It's just that I'm quite exhausted," he said, trying to hide his embarrassment.

Keeper of Secrets

"Not at all," interjected the Night Watchman. "I believe that you've had quite a day. Perhaps it's time for you to return to your hotel and get some rest. Besides, I can't expect you to keep my schedule. I'll be up past dawn. It will be morning before I take my rest. We have covered much already, yet there is more. You must meet me again tomorrow night, and we will continue." With that, he got up, walked over to the hut and disappeared inside.

Raj got up and stretched long and hard, getting his blood flowing and limbering up his body for the hike back to the hotel. He could only think that his meeting with this rare being was truly a blessing. He knew literally nothing about the Night Watchman–who he was, where he was from, or for that matter, what his name was. What he did know was that he was in the presence of a remarkable man who was privileged to be the bearer of great wisdom. This wisdom spanned the millennia and gave clarity and focus to some of the most enduring mysteries of the ages. Was the Night Watchman's knowledge real and correct? Was his authority genuine and divinely inspired? Raj would have to wait to find out more. What he did know was that the teaching rang true in his heart, and he always followed his heart.

Mohammed was restless and tired from his long day's "work." Raj sensed this and said, "Mohammed, you have served me well. How can I repay you?"

"Well, Mr. Raj, how about one hundred dollars U.S., please?"

Raj was taken aback. One hundred U.S. dollars seemed like an awful lot of money for services offered as a favor, especially with the exchange rate of three to one. Besides, Raj was expected to negotiate the offer. "How about fifty Egyptian pounds? I hope that's O.K. because, it's all I've got."

Mohammed acquiesced to the fifty pounds, and they headed down the plateau. He escorted Raj to the hotel where he took his leave. His parting words were: "If you ever need another guide just call for Mohammed." Never mind where or how to call, Raj thought amused, the call was enough. Eventually, someone named

Mohammed would appear, to be a guide.

He went up to his room and, despite his exhaustion, was ready to enter as much of what he could remember of the evening's events into his journal. He thought it would be best to get it down in writing while it was still fresh in his mind.

Entering his room, he turned on the light to find the bed already occupied. He was pleasantly surprised to find Tamera already sound asleep–unexpected but not unappreciated. It didn't take him long to reconsider his idea of adding journal entries. It was 4 a.m. he was dog-tired, and Tamera lay in his bed. Careful to not wake her up, he stripped and collapsed on the bed, quickly falling into a deep sleep, the sleep of those who have given their all.

Keeper of Secrets

Chapter 10

The 'Cairo'

It was 10 a.m. when Raj was awakened by a gentle nudge to his side. He turned slowly to find Tamera already up, with breakfast in place on a room-service cart. The smell of fresh coffee and scrambled eggs filled the room. Tamera was wearing a white terry-cloth robe tied loosely at the waist. She made no effort to conceal her voluptuous body.

"Sabah al-khair, good morning my love," she melodically intoned, "I hope you don't mind my being here. A manager friend gave me a pass key. I couldn't resist waiting here for you."

"It's the best surprise I could have hoped for. You look beautiful," Raj responded, not completely awake.

She leaned over and gently kissed Raj passionately and he responded in kind. Their tender affection led to more vigorous play and soon they were enmeshed in each other's loving embrace, stopping intermittently to eat eggs, toast and jam, which they playfully fed to each other. They lingered together for several hours enjoying each moment. Raj told Tamera about the Night Watchman and all that had happened since he was dropped off at the Sphinx. She listened, intrigued by his story.

"I've heard of a secret brotherhood, the keepers of an ancient wisdom," Tamera revealed. "There have been stories of their presence, but I've never met anyone connected to them, or who even claimed to know them. He seems like a fascinating man, this Night Watchman. Will you get to see him again?"

"Yes, he asked me to return tonight. I'm looking forward to it. He has great wisdom and probably a lot more to say. He's certainly someone you should meet. Would you like to come with me?"

"Yes, I'd be delighted. Are you sure it's all right?"

"I can't imagine why not. Besides, he has a message that must be shared, especially with someone as lovely as you!"

"I'd love to come with you," Tamera said, visibly excited.

"I plan to go later, after dark. Until then, we have the whole day together."

"Good", Tamera affirmed, "because I was hoping to take you to the Cairo Museum. It's a treasure house of Egyptian antiquities, and I'm well acquainted with the collection. My father used to take me there when I was a young girl. He would tell me stories about the glorious days of the pharaon. Actually, there are many mysterious objects there that will expand your understanding of ancient Egypt. Perhaps I can be your tour guide?"

"Nothing would please me more. Anyway, I was hoping to spend more time with you."

"There is always a way, if the heart speaks clearly enough. But, you must ask."

Raj looked deeply into her eyes, and said with sincerity, "My heart speaks more clearly than ever before. It says 'be with me'."

"Then I will!" she said, lovingly.

Raj was grateful for her understanding. She had shown him tenderness and love. A chemistry had formed between them, and their hearts had opened to eachother. He could feel their relationship growing. What started as an innocent attraction had become a stream of affection with feelings flowing as deep as the Nile itself.

It was, for Raj, a defining moment in his journey. Although gratified by his profound spiritual experiences, he felt a mystical awakening taking place within his heart. It was an awakening to a love that transcended the self, a love beyond the bounds of time or even of the body. It was a love emanating from the soul.

"Let's get started. There is much to see," implored Tamera.

Raj agreed, and they got dressed and left the hotel through a side exit, avoiding the questioning eyes of her fellow co-workers. They walked two blocks toward the city and grabbed a taxicab to Tahrir Square, a bustling commercial area in the heart of Cairo.

The 'Cairo'

The museum was one block from the square and another block from the Nile, whose cooling breezes could be felt as they walked down the street toward the museum.

Raj was excited to be going to the Cairo Museum again. He was interested not only in the artifacts and treasures of Egypt's civilization, but in the people themselves–how they lived, what they thought, and who they were. Books were plentiful on the subject, but the experience of being at the museum was much more revealing.

Nowhere in the world is the history of a single culture as represented as it is in the Cairo Museum. Only in a walk through the 'Cairo' can each step carry you through thousands of years of history. These years were defined by the passing of great pharaohs whose reigns were based on traditions of monument-building and a strong belief in the hereafter. So deeply rooted were their beliefs that how they died was as important as how they lived.

From the moment he reached the courtyard of the museum, Raj could sense a distinct energy. Strewn about the courtyard garden were monumental objects that most western museums would proudly showcase in places of honor and distinction. Ancient obelisks stood casually beside columns inscribed with hieroglyphics resting on plain stone platforms. Sphinxes sat by flagstone pathways interrupted by occasional Acacia trees, while pharaohs and their favorite goddesses stood frozen in mid-step, as if alive. Closer to the museum's outer walls, blocks of carved granite lay in unkept piles, waiting for proper display. Raj had the feeling that once a stone made it to the garden it was there to stay, a final resting place for objects that could no longer fit into the cramped confines of the museum's inner holds. He reveled in the garden's antiquities, especially because he could touch and feel the stones, caress the statues and trace the hieroglyphs with his fingers to his heart's content.

"Raj, your enjoyment thrills me, but I think you'll be even happier inside. That's where the real treasures are displayed."

Keeper of Secrets

Tamera was right, he thought, but the day was still young. Raj checked his camera bag at the door, at the insistence of the museum guard, and they went inside. He could have baksheeshed the guard into letting the camera through, but he thought it better to be unencumbered by the camera so he could focus on the artifacts themselves. Besides, the gift shop had plenty of good photos for sale.

Entering the Cairo Museum was like walking into the belly of a great whale that had just swallowed most of the world's antiquities. Raj was overwhelmed by its dimensions and its vast quantity of artifacts. Perfectly carved basalt statues and row upon row of sarcophagi were interspersed with cases of finely crafted objects of every possible description.

There were sarcophagi from every dynasty and for every occasion. They came in different shapes and sizes spanning the gamut from plain to extremely ornate. There were sarcophagi that fit inside sarcophagi that fit into still others, six deep. They were made of black granite, red granite, green granite, limestone, diorite, and heavily embellished wood. Each sarcophagus was opulently adorned with precious metals and stones such as gold, silver, lapis lazuli, malachite, turquoise, carnelian and jet. They were ornamented in exquisite inlays, depicting patterns of dress and features that must have required lifetimes of artistic endeavor to execute. The Museum was truly a mummy's delight.

The ancient Egyptians must have appreciated a good sarcophagus the way modern man appreciates a good automobile. However, only the wealthy could realize the dream of owning such a conveyance, because calculating the proporton of the total number of sarcophagi found (some thousands) to the general population thought to have lived in the Nile Valley over the millennia (some hundreds of millions), only a small percentage of the population was actually able to ride one of these sleek stone chariots into eternity.

Though the museum's collection abounded with artifacts from

The 'Cairo'

every aspect of Egyptian life, it was the giant statuary dedicated to the pharaohs that was most striking. Tamera led Raj through the main hall past a giant pink-granite head of the Fifth Dynasty pharaoh Userkef. His eyes appeared frozen, a tacit stare through the far reaches of time.

"Look at the shape and proportion of this head. The pharaonic sculptors had mastered the technique of working in a larger-than-life style," she said matter-of-factly.

"Tamera, could you lead me to statues of the pharaohs of the Giza pyramids?"

"Yes, I'd be delighted to show you."

They proceeded out of the main hall through a labyrinth of special rooms, each dedicated to the cache of a different historical period. They were headed for Room 42, where masterpieces of the Fourth Dynasty were kept. In a small niche along a wall stood the finely crafted statue of the Pharaoh Menkaure. He was the pharaoh associated with the third pyramid. Made of finely polished green schist, Menkaure was standing in a striding position flanked by the Goddess Hathor on one side and another local goddess on the other. Menkaure was in good company.

Upon entering Room 42, Tamera led Raj to a statue of the Pharaoh Khaphre. A marvel to behold, Khaphre's likeness was crafted in extremely hard, black diorite. It depicts him seated on his throne with his head cradled by the wings of a falcon, the symbol of Horus. His headdress, folded and swept back behind his ears, follows the Osirian dress code, a style of unknown origin first appearing on the Great Sphinx. His strong bearded chin and perfectly formed eyes stare off into eternity. His physical anatomy, muscular and balanced, portray a man in the prime of his power.

"But what of Khufu? Surely his pyramid was the greatest of the three Giza pharaohs. Is there an image of him as well?" Raj inquired.

"Of Khufu, there is only a small, three inch ivory statuette," she replied.

Keeper of Secrets

"But why would the pharaoh associated with the greatest monument in the history of Egypt not have a substantial likeness created in his memory?" Raj asked in earnest. "He must have been an extremely powerful pharaoh."

"This is one of the unsolved mysteries of the ancients," Tamera responded sincerely. "I honestly don't know."

Raj wondered about this enigma and was certain others had asked the same question.

"Let me take you to see some special artifacts. Although they are generally less understood, these objects are quite fascinating." She led Raj by the hand out of Room 42 to the collections of the Middle Kingdoms.

They walked past numerous cabinets filled with hundreds of small funerary statuettes called Ushabti, which were placed in the coffins of mummies to do the work of the dead. These statuettes have always been popular with tourists, and a small cottage industry had developed around their manufacture. They were created utilizing the time-honored formula, "made new to look old." In fact, the museum gift shop had an excellent selection of mummy-like pieces whose raised hieroglyphic surfaces retained the ingrained dirt that presumably gave them the look of antiquity. Amazing, Raj thought, what a piece of perfectly new ceramic can turn into when buried in dirt and drenched in camel piss.

They entered the Middle Kingdom room, which was down the hall from the Old Kingdom room and filled with countless artifacts including those of the twelfth dynasty pharaohs. Among these was the curious *Benben stone* of Amenemhet III, known to be almost four thousand years old.

"The Benben Stone was an important religious artifact of the early dynasties," Tamera articulated. She seemed to know quite a bit about the ancient history of her remarkable country. Raj was a willing student and accepted her knowledge and insight. "From the earliest times," she continued, "the original Benben Stone was kept in the Holy of Holies at the Temple of the Phoenix at Innu, also

The 'Cairo'

called Heliopolis, the sacred city of light. It was placed at the apex of a long rough stone column and was thought to have been a meteor fragment whose form had been tapered from its fiery entry into the earth's atmosphere. Although it was known to have disappeared eons ago, the original was said to have cosmic powers and was considered an especially sacred object. It was believed that meteors, or shooting stars, were signs from the gods, evidence of their heavenly intervention with man. You may know that within the most holy shrine of Islam, the *Ka'bah* in Mecca, is also a large black stone thought to be a meteorite. Some ancient records suggest that fiery meteors were considered to be semen of gods, sent earthward to seed their god-like qualities among humankind. The original Benben Stone became the prototype of the obelisks that followed. Each obelisk was capped by the characteristic four-sided form, which was also used to cap the larger pyramid structures. This fine example from the time of Amenemhet III bears some rather interesting inscriptions. Take a closer look."

Raj observed two rows of hieroglyphic inscriptions around the lower base of the polished black granite, capstone. The base measured about three feet on each side and tapered to a slightly chipped point. On one side, above the hieroglyphic writing, was the symbol of Ra, the solar disk surrounded by the double Uraeus (two cobras enwrapping the sun), and fanning out from that were two distinct wings, arched downward. Curiously centered under the wings were two human eyes, much like ones seen on Buddhist stupas in Nepal. Under the wings was a line of hieroglyphic writing containing the pharaoh's cartouches which straddled another sun disk and was framed by ankhs (the symbol of eternal life).

"I believe you might be especially interested in this little figure." Tamera said, pointing to a small humanoid figure whose outstretched arm held a star. "This is the symbol of Osiris/Sahu, the aspect of Osiris associated with the constellation of Orion. This pharaoh was part of the Osirian brotherhood and understood the relationship to the stars."

Keeper of Secrets

Raj began to think of his visit to the museum as an extension of his immersion into the arcane teachings.

"Let me take you to look at some special stelae," Tamera suggested. She seemed adamant about this, and led Raj firmly by the arm.

"These old stones must really be important."

"It's not the stones that are important, although most are marvelous to behold; it's the stories they tell that make them important. These stones, you see, are not silent."

She led Raj into a small, dimly lit room at the end of a long corridor. The room seemed like an afterthought to the museum's layout, since it was small enough to have been an office. Entering the room, Raj noticed that the room was strangely empty. He had the feeling that he was being treated to a private showing. An eerie quiet pervaded the room as they walked across it. Lined up against the walls was a collection of hieroglyphically inscribed stones, varying in height from several inches to several feet. Some were displayed on pedestals, the broken chunks of larger monoliths. Others were encased in simple, oak-framed glass cabinets requiring just the right angle of sight to be viewed without any obscuring glare.

The stelae were made of different materials ranging from red, hard-polished granite, to pale, soft limestone. Each exhibited distinct patterns of wear and erosion. These stones were notable because of the information conveyed on their hard chiseled surfaces, information that, however fragmented or partially obscured by age and abuse, told a fascinating tale. Most important were the cartouches that covered many of them.

"These are the names of the pharaohs written down for posterity as a record of the ruling lineage going back to the First Time, called by the Egyptians *'Zep Tepi'*. If we are to believe these stelae and the dates contained on them, the epoch of pharaohs and the earlier god-kings dates back into pre-history. This piece on the left is called the Palermo Stone. It's called that because it is one of three fragments of a larger stone monolith whose largest fragment is in a museum in Palermo, Italy. When taken as a whole, the hieroglyphs detail a time before recorded history when rulers who were called the *Venerables* and the *Shemsu-Hor* ruled Egypt. It says that the Venerables reigned for 23,200 years and the Shemsu-Hor (translated as the follower of Horus) ruled for 13,420 years. If we trust in the validity of these figures, they suggest that these god-like rulers of pre-history were around for more years than conceived as possible in the currently accepted historical model.

"Raj, look at this limestone rectangle. It's called the Inventory Stela. It states that the Sphinx and the pyramids are much older than previously thought. This is in line with the discovery of Dr. Ali that we witnessed at Saqqara. These stelae, however, are not being interpreted in this way by Egyptologists. They seem to think that these earlier epochs are only ambiguous inferences. They regard the First Dynasty and its founding by the Pharaoh Menes as the beginning of Egypt. Menes united the northern and southern kingdoms around the year 3,100 BC, or a little over five thousand years ago. Before that, the inhabitants of Egypt were considered to be primitives."

"Again, evidence of a greater antiquity for the history of humankind," Raj offered.

"Exactly. In fact, the Inventory Stela dedicates the Great Pyramid to the Goddess Isis as 'Mistress of the Pyramid' and indicates the existence of the pyramids long before the Pharaoh Khufu."

"It seems that our understanding of the origins of the ancient world needs some re-thinking."

"There seems to be plenty of evidence; it's really a matter of interpretation."

Raj nodded in agreement. He realized that these odd-shaped remnants of a highly-skilled, stone-working society were becoming important pieces in a modern jig-saw puzzle, one containing a profound insight about who we are and where we come from.

Keeper of Secrets

After a moment of silent contemplation Tamera turned to Raj, suggesting, "Let's go and see the treasures of Tutenkhamun. They're on the second floor, an exhibit not to be missed."

They bolted up the adjoining marble staircase and down another long hallway. They were headed for Room 4. The presence of several armed guards indicated that they were getting close to something valuable. The security detail consisted of two guards stationed outside the entrance to the Tutenkhamun room and two inside the room. Except for the menacing presence of their M-16 rifles, the room lacked any other kind of security.

Undeniably, the most exquisite artifacts in the Cairo Museum are those belonging to the Pharaoh Tutenkhamun. They are on display in an ordinary room, contained in simple glass cabinets. Considering the priceless nature of the treasures of the young pharaoh, Raj was surprised to see the jewelry, and especially the famous golden funerary mask, displayed so simply. Single paned glass with no alarms or other precautions separated the casual observer from the treasures. The golden mask of Tutenkhamun, perhaps the most priceless Egyptian relic ever discovered, was on display with no more formality than ordinary cobbler's tools. Raj was happy to get close to the treasures without the usual high-tech security barriers that separate the viewer from the viewed.

The mask is an object of extraordinary craftsmanship. The golden visage of the young pharaoh, frozen in gilded relief, was perfectly proportioned with balanced delicate features. Tutenkhamun's mask is a molten snapshot congealed in time, idealizing the departed, youthful king. The other objects in adjoining cases were also treasures, each perfect in their own right. Displayed was a king's ransom of fine jewelry: necklaces, bracelets, armbands and other adornments that accompanied the pharaoh into eternity.

They left the museum satiated from the feast of ancient artifacts. The glory that was once Egypt faded as they re-entered the real world of modern Cairo. By contrast, the surrounding aging apartment buildings had none of the regal dignity that was evident in the temple structures of old. At best, they reminded Raj of the apartment blocks of New York City–old and worn.

The Nile gleamed in the afternoon sun as they walked toward the adjacent promenade. On a whim, Raj leapt into one of the colorful fellucas moored at the river's edge, Tamera following him. He negotiated a fair price with the lean, turbaned boat operator for a short sail out on the river. Within moments they were drawn into the river's flow by sails billowing in the breezes racing along the cool surface waters. It was a blissful romantic interlude, a sweet moment to be savored as they tacked against the river, heading south.

Back at the hotel, Tamera lingered with Raj but soon left for work. Raj decided to relax for the rest of the day, planning to meet again with the Night Watchman later that evening. Strolling down to the pool he grabbed a lounge cushion, sat down and ordered a drink. He lay back to rest, slowly sipping a White Russian and looked out in awe at the panorama before him. Reflected in the shimmering hotel pool was the Great Pyramid.

KEEPER OF SECRETS

Chapter 11

THE SACRED MISSION

Raj and Tamera arrived at the pyramids as the first stars pierced the velvet veil of indigo night, their scintillating projections visible through the unfathomable depths of black space, boundless time and quivering atmosphere. Night fell swiftly as they walked along Pyramid Road, using the remaining radiance of twilight to facilitate their passage. They made their way to the hut of the Night Watchman, aided by a small flashlight which barely illuminated the narrow trail.

Temple wall outcroppings cast shadowy forms around them as they passed. In the distance they could see a friendly fire like a candle in a window guiding their way home.

Raj was welcomed joyously by the Night Watchman who was already seated by the fire. Introducing Tamera, Raj sat down and settled into a half-lotus position, one leg folded over the other. Tamera sat beside him in silent anticipation.

"I have been expecting you," the Night Watchman said, with evident foresight.

"Then you knew I'd be bringing a guest?" Raj asked.

"Yes. To fulfill my mission I must pass the teaching to both of you. You have been brought here for this noble purpose; your lives bound together for this purpose."

The Night Watchman passed around glasses of freshly-poured tea. Raj quietly began a series of cleansing breaths, gazing at the fire and the shifting patterns of flames, drawing himself into a trance. The fire's glowing embers transformed into cities of light, changing often as the crumbling fuel disintegrated into ash.

The Night Watchman cleared his throat and began to speak, "I extend my heart-felt gratitude, for you have made your way here to receive the wisdom that I must impart. Your presence will assist me in my mission, for as this knowledge is passed to you, so must you pass it to others. May you live long in the light of Ra, and may Ra's radiance bless you in all your days."

Raj was deeply touched by this pronouncement and responded, "My dear friend, I am here to fulfill my sacred duty as a servant of the whole. In the name of Ra and the Holy Mother Isis, may I do my part."

"And I, too, seek to serve the Holy Mother Isis," Tamera earnestly offered, "that I may bring the teaching to my people, inheritors of this land, and to women everywhere."

"Yes, this is right and just," the Night Watchman affirmed. "Then we can begin. For now I wish to recount an astounding legend, one that is woven through history and the lives of many peoples over vast stretches of time. It carries with it the thread of concordant consciousness, a living legacy whose vibrancy and meaning have been preserved even unto this day.

"Since the dawn of memory, before the beginning of the pharaonic line of god-kings, the Brotherhood of Ra was entrusted with the sacred mission of preserving the eternal knowledge. In this way, the living flame of truth was preserved through the ages, handed down in an unbroken chain from teacher to student, adept to neophyte. These sacred teachings contain the wisdom of the Elder Brothers, those beyond the veil of death, and constitute the 'Opening of the Way' for entry onto the path of higher evolution.

"Embodied in the teachings is a record of all that is known about the origin of consciousness, a body of knowledge so important and so crucial to the development of humanity that the priests entrusted to uphold its preservation were sworn to their sacred task under penalty of death.

"The timeless knowledge of the ancients revealed the nature of the spirit and taught the alignment of the soul, mind and body–the keys to unlocking the inner potential of being. It was through this knowledge that they sought to facilitate the unfoldment of divine

THE SACRED MISSION

powers within every human being. They understood how to accelerate spiritual development and taught the path of the heart and of compassion. They were adept in the science of sound and utilized sacred words and prayers, communicating beyond the veil of death and directly with the forces of nature. They were masters of the science of inner sight and were able to see into the past and the future. They also practiced the healing arts and mastered techniques for reading and transmitting thought.

"They based their work on the science of breath and used the breath to enhance consciousness. By this method they mastered awareness, achieved conscious death and rebirth, and maintained dominion over destiny." The Night Watchman paused in a moment of reflection.

Raj was enthralled by the Night Watchman's knowledge. He could only hope to be a worthy vessel for such an exalted teaching. Still, there was much to understand and his mind was filled with questions. "How was the knowledge passed along?" he asked.

"Transmitting and protecting the sacred teaching was a sworn duty of the Brotherhood. Much of what was taught was passed down by oral tradition, with each generation learning the codified teachings. This required a special training to condition the memory.

"The enlightened teachers instructed their students in the technique of extended awareness, focusing on extending the length of time consciousness could be maintained while entering into, and coming out of, sleep. Gradually, presence of mind was preserved consistently, in and out of the dream state. This practice developed control in all states of being and helped establish awareness separate from the body. By being active on the inner planes, the students became awakened to their soul.

"From an early age each student had to pass through difficult tests designed to gauge their abilities. These tests were known as initiations and were an important part of the learning process. Slowly, the neophytes would advance in skill until they demonstrated continuous awareness. By this act they could preserve their accumulated knowledge through all states of being. They were then consecrated 'Awakened Ones', and had the responsibility to preserve and guard the ancient wisdom. These Awakened Ones founded the mystery schools and established the Brotherhood of Ra.

"Through practicing 'continuity of consciousness' they activated the 'sacred silver thread' (linking the soul's incarnations like pearls on a string) and were able to preserve the purity of wisdom handed down from generation to generation. After death, the Awakened Ones were reborn, picking up where they left off in their previous life. In this way, they were able to watch over the dissemination of the sacred teaching, ensuring its proper transmission."

"If the Awakened Ones reincarnated to preserve the teaching, what role did the students play?"

"Those neophytes who succeeded in assimilating the teachings became carriers of the seeds of wisdom. They had a sacred duty to cultivate those seeds within humanity. It was from the cultivation of a spirit-conscious humanity that the Awakened Ones hoped to produce a majestic civilization where every man, woman and child could walk the holy path to God, producing a heaven on earth. This shining manifestation would be a beacon of light for the world, illuminating the ages and establishing a time of love and goodness which, they hoped, would last unto eternity.

"And so the Brotherhood of Ra maintained their presence guiding human evolution. In many ways they were successful in their efforts and their society flourished, leading to a golden age."

Raj was trying to put the images together so that he could picture the entire story. He inquired, "Where did these great teachers come from?"

The Night Watchman paused, as if to frame the question in his mind, then thoughtfully responded, "The answer to this question is one that may astound you, because it will forever change your understanding of the origin of human civilization. Let me explain.

"Before recorded history, great illumined teachers walked freely among humankind. Their presence was a beneficent force that guided our development. Then a devastating planetary cataclysm swept the earth, decimating the world's population and leaving only a remnant of society to carry on. The great teachers returned to help rebuild civilization. It was a time called by the ancients 'Zep Tepi' or The New Beginning."

"I've heard of this Zep Tepi from my father," suggested Tamera. "Can you explain this in more detail?"

"Yes, of course. There was, some 12,500 years ago, a global disaster that abruptly ended the last ice age. It was caused by a shift of the earth's crust and was accompanied by massive floods from the quick meltdown of the polar ice caps. Stories of these floods are found in the legends and mythologies of nations and peoples the world over."

"But, how could this have happened? What could have caused such a disaster?" questioned Raj.

"That is a very important question. The cataclysm was caused by the movement of the outer crust of the earth around the molten inner layer that lies between the crust and the solid central core. This movement is regarded as a pole-shift, because the poles appear to shift. In fact, the poles stay the same–it's the earth's crust that shifts position. This phenomenon was caused by a confluence of circumstances, including the earth's axial wobble, alignments of the sun, moon and planets (causing extreme gravitational tides), a destabilization of the earth's magnetic field (due to violent solar storms), and the build-up of the polar ice caps.

"A shift of the relatively thin outer crust of the earth was set in motion by centrifugal forces and the massive weight of the polar ice caps. In any revolving spherical body, mass wants to displace toward the outer circumference of the sphere. In the case of our earth, mass accumulated at the poles would tend to move toward the equator. This is usually prevented by the magnetic coupling of the earth's outer crust to the inner viscous layer. When the crust became uncoupled (due to a massive solar storm that neutralized the earth's magnetic field), the weight of the polar ice caps caused the movement of the outer crust, as is to be expected by natural physical laws. This placed the former poles in more temperate climates inducing a rapid meltdown of the ice caps (and consequently the mythic biblical floods), while thrusting temperate lands into the freezing polar regions, causing rapid glaciation in those areas. This is a cycle that has happened before in geological history and will, one day, happen again."

"But wouldn't the effects of such massive destruction be evident?" Raj questioned.

"Yes. In fact, evidence of this cataclysm can still be seen, even though the force of the devastation was severe enough to eliminate most traces of human civilization. There exist, for example, remains of large herds of now extinct animals buried in northern Alaska and Siberia. Their bones and flesh were flash frozen and preserved in the tundra permafrost. Whole mastodons have been found, frozen solid, with meals of buttercups (a flower of the temperate regions) still in their stomachs!

"We also know that the continent of Antarctica, first 'discovered' in 1818, and having been under two miles of polar ice-pack for many thousands of years, was once a fertile, temperate land, completely free of ice. Ancient maps have been found, such as the Piri Reis map of 1513, which clearly show the coast line of Antarctica as it was before it was covered by ice. These maps indicate knowledge of a pre-glaciated Antarctic continent, yet the scientific skill to penetrate the ice cover has only recently been possible and was first shown in a seismic survey by a French research team during a 1957 Geophysical Year project.

"There is even evidence of a climatic shift in the layers of snow deposited on the island of Greenland. A recent scientific expedition sent to examine core samples drilled deep into Greenland's ice sheet and uncovered a snow layer deposited some 12,500 years ago, indicating an extreme change in climate. Within a single season, the snow-fall over Greenland increased dramatically and has remained that way ever since. Analyses reveal a different type of snow caused by the high moisture content found in the air of a warmer climate. A radical climate change of this nature points to a dislocation of the earth's surface."

"So you're saying that a shift of the earth's crust, or pole-shift, wiped out humanity in the distant past?"

"Indeed. The destruction caused by this planetary re-orientation was felt throughout the world and was quite complete in its devastation. Of course, this left the remnants of humanity to sort things out. They had to begin the long climb toward a viable civilization, but they were not alone.

"After the crustal shakeup subsided and its repercussions ended, the survivors of the cataclysm, without the support of their societies, reverted to a barbaric existence. Then a group of divinely inspired beings appeared who helped the survivors to develop a new civilization. When they appeared, they were thought to be gods. The knowledge, compassion and assistance provided by these enlightened beings engendered solemn respect and veneration. They were representatives of the Brotherhood of Ra, men and women distinguished by their spiritual advancement and entrusted with the task of guiding humanity through the long march toward a renewed civilization.

"They traced their lineage to the far older 'Atlantean' civilization which inhabited the world prior to the great destruction. They were the builders of the Sphinx and were responsible for establishing the foundation of the modern human race. If it were not for their tireless efforts over such vast periods of time, humanity might still be primitive hunter-gatherers, or worse–cannibalistic barbarians."

"So, the survivors of the last cataclysm were guided toward developing a new civilization?" Raj asked.

"Yes, this is so. Without this assistance, developing an organized society would have taken much longer. Not only did they help establish a new society, they also planned to leave a record of their experiences and a warning for future generations. "

"This is most intriguing," Raj offered. "Please, explain this."

"It came to pass that a plan was devised to build a monument that would last throughout the ensuing millennia. This monument would mark the position of the earth's surface after the crustal shift stabilized, indicating the point where true north was fixed. They decided to construct a structure that would last the test of time, a structure that would always be noticed and revered. They chose the pyramid and planned its construction near the site of an earlier monument: the Sphinx. They hoped this would be a reminder of the founding of the new civilization.

"Their plan called for building a monument which would convey their history, geophysical insights and prophesies. They encrypted into the design key mathematical information about the earth, including its precession, size and mass, axis, rotation, and its relationship to other planets and stars.

"But there was more–a hidden purpose, known only to the advanced initiates. Because of the energy-enhancements that could be realized from an application of sacred geometry, the pyramid designers constructed their monument with a solemn purpose."

"What was the true purpose of these magnificent monuments?" Raj asked intently. "Can you reveal this to us?"

"Yes, you must hear the full truth," the Night Watchman responded. His voice grew quiet, as if to convey his truth in a hushed whisper. "In essence, the pyramids served to increase the vibratory rate of the soul as it transitioned from life to after-life. The pyramids focused the soul's awareness on its celestial origin and caused an exalted state which opened the way to spiritual immortality. This was immortality achieved by continuity of consciousness, providing the soul with a means to maintain awareness whether in or out of the body. Because of this, the pyramids

THE SACRED MISSION

became known as 'Mansions of Eternity', fulfilling a sacred mission to assist the evolution of mankind. The immortality they sought was not immortal physical being, for this was counter to laws of nature, but immortality through awareness of self, maintained through the cycles of existence–death and rebirth."

"They must have had an especially advanced culture to have designed structures with such spiritual insight," Tamera suggested. "How were they able to do this?"

"The construction of the Great Pyramids fulfilled a vision that was at the very core of the Egyptian culture, a grand plan that extended thousands of years until completed. The project galvanized the entire society to join in a pious task which gave focus and meaning to their lives. The time of pyramid construction was a time of striving and discipline and the catalyst that made Egypt a great nation–one people, motivated in cooperation, and ruled by a benevolent spiritually-inspired leader.

"Egypt flourished during this accomplishment, and a great awakening occurred during the Fourth Dynasty under the reign of the Pharaoh Khufu. It was Khufu who finally completed the vision set forth in the First Time. Khufu's reign was a period of peace and prosperity when people worked together following the basic tenets of spiritual development. During this time, wonderful monuments were built consecrated to the evolution of the soul. Sciences devoted to the well-being of humanity were developed, and music, writing and other high cultural pursuits progressed. Because of the Brotherhood, the gifts of peace, prosperity and knowledge were available to all. It was truly a golden age, one dedicated to the service of humanity and the worship of the divinity in each soul, the Holy Mother Isis and the Omniscient Ra.

"It was during this time that the elements of divine worship, invocation and evocation, were brought together in perfect harmony. Not since the gods themselves walked upon the earth had such ceremonial worship been seen. But, all was not well, for a shadow loomed on the distant horizon."

"What do you mean?" Raj asked.

"At the inauguration of the first Great Pyramid a special conclave was held bringing together the most venerable sages of the Age. They came from all over the known world, from the northern and southern kingdoms of the land of Khem (the ancient name of Egypt), and from other areas that had preserved the sacred teachings. These Great Ones were linked by a bond of brotherhood woven on the subtle planes of consciousness, a mutual telepathic rapport that allowed them to communicate the vision of the evolutionary path–the Plan as it emanated from the mind of Ra."

"I've heard of this mysterious Plan," Raj said. "Supposedly it is a blueprint for human evolution."

"Yes, the Plan unfolds according to the cycles of time as expressed by the progression of Ra through the universe. The Plan formulated by Ra involves its participation in celestial consciousness and manifests as cosmic thought. This thought, once formulated, is disseminated to sensitive human co-workers–the Brotherhood of Ra.

"Because universal law allows for a limited glimpse of the future (to help with the unfoldment of the Plan), visions of the future can be accessed. They are an expression of the intent of Ra and are perceived as prophecy: the precognitive vision of those significant moments in the future whose substance has already begun to congeal as nascent thoughts in the mind of Ra."

"How was the Brotherhood able to receive this vision?" Tamera inquired.

"The combined power of the assembled seers, visionaries and high priests was harnessed to ascertain the future Plan. Utilizing telepathic meditation and other advanced techniques of thought transmission, they opened a portal of perception into the mind of Ra. Through united concentration (which acted like a focused lens), they manifested a prescient revelation. What was revealed astounded them and shook them to the core of their beings, since it produced a disturbing vision of the times to follow their 'golden age'."

"So, the future didn't look good to them," Raj commented. He seemed more than a little concerned.

"No it did not. In fact, their glorious cycle was about to come to an end. Sadly, they saw the degeneration of humanity and its slide into darkness. The descent brought greed, violence and the worship of the lower passions. Senseless acts of cruelty and inhuman behavior abounded in generation after generation. They envisioned the time in human history where the descent would reach its culmination. A time when the planetary geophysical cycle would come full circle–as it had done before.

"This disturbed the Conclave of Enlightened Souls, and they wept for the future. Their hearts were burdened by the tragic plight of those yet to be born, because they knew that through their own rebirth they would live in those times as well. They understood that there needed to be a balance in nature for a global catastrophe to be avoided. And they knew that the Great Mother, our earth, could react with devastating consequences, especially if the abuse continued unchecked.

"In vision after vision, penetrating into future ages, they foresaw humanity's terrible fate. The end of the pharaonic lineage and times of great chaos were foreseen, interrupted by occasional periods when the light would surface for a time, only to be extinguished by the resurgent madness. They saw the rape of the land and the fouling of the waters that sustained life. Suffering and pain were foreseen, with bigotry, enslavement and cruelty everywhere. They saw war on a mass scale, and man's inhumanity to man practiced in its ugliest form–genocide. Mass graves and burning cities, poisoned choking air, and the sad images of innocents stricken ill with deadly diseases pervaded their visions. They saw plagues of pestilence grown resistant to all treatment, while poisonous acids rained from the skies. Countless ages were presaged where blood spilled in the streets as neighbor fought against neighbor for domination and territory. All this and more played out before their horrified eyes."

"This is terrible!" Raj exclaimed.

"Yes, it is, but even more unsettling is that the future they saw is our own age," the Night Watchman said, consoling in his tone.

Raj was very upset and, frantically asked, "How did they deal with this horrible vision? What did they do? How did they respond?"

"With a united focus they reached into the future to determine when the rebirth of light would occur. But their visions reached an impasse beyond which it was impossible to perceive. The outcome of human destiny was tied to that moment. However, they also realized that they could impact the future, across thousands of years, through actions they could initiate in their own time.

"The nexus point was calculated to occur 4,500 years from their time, at the changing of the ages from Pisces to Aquarius. This period coincides with the present, and especially with the end of the 20th century. The Conclave understood that the thoughts and intentions of humankind would have a profound impact on the outcome of the events hidden from their sight. They also realized that a disturbance in the living continuum could be caused by a catastrophic event of global destruction which would bring humanity's progress to a halt."

"This is very disturbing!" Raj blurted out excitedly.

Tamera spoke up and in a calm manner asked, "What was their next step?"

"Troubled by their dire prophecy, they decided to create a plan to preserve the ancient wisdom, lest humanity become lost and its evolution slowed or even halted. They sought to preserve the essence of the sacred teachings for future generations, when a new era of tolerance would allow the seeds of knowledge to bloom again. The consequences of their actions were deemed so critical to the survival of humanity that a gathering of the *M'htm* was called. The M'htm were the most holy of their time, and were entrusted with invoking deity to provide the insight needed to develop a plan of action. They hoped to alter what they had seen in their dark prophetic vision.

"The M'htm decided to enact a special, rarely used ritual called the 'Vision of One Thousand Eyes', and so began fasting and praying in an effort to invoke a higher spiritual authority. They appealed to the beneficent *'Watchers'* (those souls whose advanced spiritual state had released them from the cycles of death and rebirth), seeking to receive a plan to preserve the gains made by human evolution.

"During this ritual they used sacred words of power, *hekau*, and made oblation to Ra, invoking wisdom and compassion from the deity. At the end of the ceremony, awakened from their contemplation, the great souls gathered at the foot of the newly consecrated Great Pyramid.

"Among them was the high priest Imhotep, who bore the mantle of leadership conferred by his spiritual attainment. He had guided the design of the pyramids since the time of the Pharaoh Djoser and was the builder of the Step Pyramid of Saqqara. He had attained one of the highest degrees of initiation possible for his time, and was the hierophant of the assembled hierarchy of 'Awakened Ones'. He had penetrated more deeply into the Mind of Ra than any of his brothers and had achieved complete continuity of consciousness. 'At one' with his spirit, his Aakhu, Imhotep had achieved command of sentient awareness, preserved through life and death. By his awesome power he could manifest in a body of pure light, formed by his will, yet real to the senses. He was a glory to behold, the essence of wisdom, radiating an ethereal aura of golden light.

"On that fateful day, Imhotep revealed his vision."

Keeper of Secrets

Chapter 12

THE VISION

The Night Watchman became absolutely still. His breath began to deepen so that each inhalation completely filled his lungs and each exhalation released to the fullest extent. At the end of each in-breath he paused intentionally, allowing every molecule of oxygen to seep fully into his blood. At the end of each exhalation he paused again, so that the in-rush of breath was driven by his need for air. By this action he prepared himself for entry into a receptive hypnotic trance. His eyes rolled up behind his lids, which fluttered slightly open. Quivering noticeably, as if in a state of extreme rapture, a subtle glow seemed to interpenetrate the very substance of his being. His countenance was that of a much older man radiating a profound serenity. It was clear to Raj that the Night Watchman had become overshadowed.

A spirit had imbued him with its essence, and in a slow, mesmerizing tone he uttered, "*Sa Sekhem Aakhu.* My brothers, may we be blessed by the breath, the power, and the Spirit. I am the one called Imhotep, and at this solemn moment, by our united hearts, we are in alignment with our Lord. It is our destiny, by sworn oath and divine decree, to play a crucial role in the evolution of sentient life on earth. Though we are now living in a time of peace, where humankind is striving unto light under the watchful Eye of Ra, there is much to be concerned about, for we have penetrated the future and have seen the coming ages of man.

"In the times ahead humanity must cross a vast abyss of darkness and uncertainty. Those yet unborn will descend in consciousness, becoming blind to the light of the soul. They will worship gold as their god, and the pleasures of the senses will cloud their minds. They will thirst for dominance and power resorting to oppression, violence, and terror to achieve their aims. They will not learn the lessons of compassion, kindness and forgiveness. Their hearts will grow cold in selfishness and greed, and will become like stone. They will turn upon the earth seeking only to exploit her resources for profit. In ignorance, they will poison the veil of the Mother, the thin crust of our earth that supports all life, causing illness and disease. They will take to war and acts of destruction, perfecting techniques of death and annihilation. This process will span many eons and, if unchecked, will culminate in a devastating upheaval of the earth itself.

"We must begin preparing now for this distant future. For, you see, this future is our own, as we are bound by a sacred vow to return again and again to guide the souls of humankind, establishing the path of return to our divine birthright. The wisdom we have carried and protected, through hardship and strife, must never be lost. The path must always be preserved, because the knowledge we safeguard will lead humankind out of the abyss of darkness and into light.

"We are responsible for preserving the path of light, even unto the end of time. In seeing the coming ages, we realize that Our power will become limited as the ages unfold, for the sons of men must determine their fate by their own free will; it is the law. Yet, we must be vigilant in our duty. As the human seed spreads upon the earth, we must realize that Our role will surely change. No longer will god-kings rule with absolute authority, guided by an enlightened brotherhood. No longer will we be able to work in the open, lest the sacred words of power be misused for selfish gain or senseless evil.

"To preserve the sacred wisdom we must plant the seeds of knowledge deep, realizing that actions we set in motion now may not bear fruit for millennia to come. We must also realize that only by our immediate actions can the destiny of humankind be safeguarded. An understanding of the path of divine contact and the knowledge of the human spiritual constitution must be preserved and conveyed to future generations. Imparting this wisdom will lead to the realization of divinity, and only then can all other knowledge be safely known.

"We have come to understand that the best way to accomplish this noble task is to bring the sacred teaching to a place of safekeeping in a distant land. And so, we will encode the wisdom within the words of a language to be borne upon the lips of our children and of our children's children. This language will inform all aspects of daily life, yet will preserve a deeper meaning within the roots of the most essential words. We will instruct this language to our sons and daughters, sending them forth to establish a colony in a remote, secluded and, we pray, protected part of earth. There they will live preserving the teaching until humanity is once again ready to receive the sacred wisdom.

"Our most gifted priests and scribes will create a language that will, within its essence, impart truth and spiritual knowledge. We will prepare great sailing ships capable of traversing the oceans and assemble groups of men and women to guide these vessels into the unknown. We will empower them with a sacred trust and the vision that they are the hope and future of humanity.

"I have looked into the future, through the mists of time, and have seen distant islands resplendent with tall mountains and draped with lush, emerald green forests. Bejeweled are these islands with exotic flowers of every hue and scent and with the sign of the rainbow everywhere to be seen. This paradise of gentle climate and lush fertility is surrounded by a warm, crystal clear ocean filled with abundant life. Endowed with clean fresh streams and many varieties of fruits, herbs, and plants, this island paradise will provide sustenance and support for the ensuing generations.

"This envisioned land is a string of volcanic islands that have formed in a vast, distant ocean, isolated from all other lands. Its mountains are alive and still bear witness to the fiery forces of generation. It lies in a zone of safety, protected by its position from any dislocations or shifting of the earth's surface. Because of this, it will serve as a preserve, a living ark, throughout the years to come.

"Many generations of our brave descendants will seek this promised land, and many of those who undertake the journey will never arrive. For this reason, we shall enlist those souls who have been tested in the fire of life and found to be endowed with patience, perseverance and courage. We will send out a number of expeditionary groups, all with the same goal–to find the envisioned land and, upon arrival, to thrive and develop a new society, preserving the seeds of the sacred wisdom.

"I have called this land H'w' and have placed within its name a special key to the secret meaning imbedded in its essence. For this is a land born of fire and water, blessed with the sekhem of the creator, and resplendent with the veil of the Mother. It is there that we shall safely keep the seed of divine consciousness and knowledge of the chord that connects the seed to the source. It is there, within the cradle of paradise, that the sacred teaching shall be preserved."

As the spirit of Imhotep quietly faded, the Night Watchman slumped in his seat. He appeared spent and lapsed into sleep. Raj saw the strain that maintaining the spirit of an exalted soul had caused, and decided it was best to leave him alone.

He got up and stretched his legs, mildly cramped from their crossed position, and went to re-invigorate the fire, which had burned down to ashen coals. Adding a handful of wooden splinters, he leaned close to the fire and began blowing on the coals. He was comforted by the fire's magic power, feeling in its transitory nature an apt metaphor for his feelings of insignificance in the face of the fate of the world. Tamera sat in silence with her eyes closed.

In time, the Night Watchman opened his eyes and breathed a long sigh. He brought his hands to his face and rubbed his eyes, as if to terminate the visitation. With his large, gnarled hands he lifted an old, blackened tea-kettle onto the fire.

The Vision

A desert wind blew gently from the north, accentuating the mystical ambiance with a thrilling sensation.

"As you can see, the Ancient Ones are with us," the Night Watchman affirmed, "even as we sit here in the deep of night. And so it was in the time of Imhotep, who spoke through me so that you may understand that the future was foretold, and actions were taken to safeguard the ancient wisdom. This was the inception of a sacred mission, a mission that continues even unto this day."

Raj was speechless, savoring the residual energy that emanated from the visitation. All he could do was take it all in.

"In that momentous time," the Night Watchman continued, "great sailing ships were built to transport the explorers into the vast unknown. They sailed to the far reaches of the oceans to the east, where few had gone before. The explorers were instructed to travel beyond the horizon, sailing toward the rising sun. Their destination would be found by following the sacred prophecy as indicated by certain heavenly signs.

"Their ships were loaded with the provisions and tools necessary to start a new life, for they knew their journey was a one-way excursion. The expeditionary groups were composed of men and women chosen for their compatibility. Each vessel had crew members with a broad range of skills necessary for survival. They were dependent on each other, which required complete cooperation and trust.

"They were instructed in the newly-developed language and become fluent in its use, for they were required to speak it and no other until it became second-nature to them.

"The language was created by the most learned minds of the time. The ancient Egyptians were masters at developing linguistic structures, encoding meaning on a number of levels. In fact, their hieroglyphic alphabet provided both a lettered sound and a pictographic image, where each image revealed a subtle thought that, when taken together, formed words that articulated complex insights. The words were organized into sentences which were composed into sacred prayers or 'spells'. The meanings of the underlying images revealed a storehouse of knowledge apparent only to the initiated. By concealing the secret wisdom within their writing, they were able to protect it from profanation and misuse.

"For this sacred mission, their scholars developed a spoken language designed to achieve a similar encrypting effect, without a written alphabet. Each word had an outward significance, but it could also be broken down into separate root words expressing a hidden meaning. These root words were then linked together to reveal the teaching. They composed sacred prayers and epic legends which communicated the teachings when plumbed for the underlying meaning. These prayers were committed to memory to ensure their survival.

"The ancients had achieved remarkable proficiency in the development of memory and were able to memorize prayers consisting of hundreds of verses. Each could be recalled word for word in an perpetual stream of recollection. The prayers were passed as a sacred trust from generation to generation in an unbroken tradition. This required the cultivation of focused attention, which was developed to a heightened level. The mastery of this mental power became an important aspect of their lives.

"As long as the lineage continued and the language carried on, the teaching would be preserved, embedded in the language. This assured its safekeeping without concern for the deterioration or loss of written records. Records engraved in heavy stone or written on delicate papyrus would not survive a long ocean voyage. The entrusted explorers themselves would become the repositories of the teachings.

"There was a grand ceremony on the day the fleet set sail. Emotions ran high as loved ones said their farewells, knowing they would never see each other again. The migration began with twelve ships, each laden with the precious cargo of knowledge–the living seed of the future. Each group was organized as a separate whole whose mission would continue despite the fate of the others.

The Vision

"There was no turning back as the ships sailed south through the Red Sea past upper Egypt and Nubia, through the Gulf of Aden, and out into the vastness of the Indian ocean. They plotted their course guided by the path of the sun by day and the stars at night, according to the instructions of Imhotep's vision. They used their rapport with the elements to fill their sails with wind, and knowledge of the natural ocean currents that swirl and flow in streams across the earth, to carry their boats onward. They carefully studied and memorized complex star charts, developing the skills necessary for trans-oceanic navigation.

"Imhotep's vision had revealed a string of un-inhabited islands in the far Pacific, half-way around the world. So remote was their location that the outward migration of other peoples had not reached their shores. The islands were a natural preserve, untouched and unspoiled since the beginning of time.

"These envisioned islands are now called Hawai'i. The original settlers were descendants of the ancient Egyptians who began their journey some five thousand years ago. Their migration was to touch many lands, and at each stop along the way they conveyed the sacred teaching, shedding light on the path wherever they landed. Some of the expeditionary vessels found distant landings and new missions that compelled them to remain, abandoning the quest in order to help the local inhabitants. This was the case in India, Burma and Indonesia. Today, temples embracing the ancient code still grace these lands, as is the case in Borobudur and Bali. And in India the beneficent Ra is still worshipped as Ram.

"In the fullness of time, the generations moved eastward, the mission of reaching the 'promised paradise' always foremost in their hearts and minds. Eventually there appeared on the distant horizon emerald green peaks rising out of the curving oceanic surface. There, within a cleft in the mist-enshrouded mountains, a translucent rainbow arched above a sheer lava cliff. This was the sign they sought to tell them they had arrived, a sign prophesied by the ancient vision. This spot was made into a shrine, for its energies had penetrated through the years to guide their way 'home'. Their arrival was a great triumph for the light, because it brought the sacred teaching into the bosom of the Mother and into guarded safety.

"As their society developed under the guidance of the sacred teaching, a distinct culture emerged evolving parallel to the rest of the world. It was based on the wisdom implicit in their language and on the nature and purity of their new home land. They would, in fact, develop their culture based on 'existence in paradise', a paradigm whose expression allowed them to live in simple harmony with nature, yet achieve an understanding of human consciousness that far surpassed other cultures.

"Now I must reveal to you the secret of the hidden teaching. Hidden within the words of a gentle people by a wise and noble race at the dawn of understanding."

Chapter 13

OF KA, BA AND AAKHU

The Night Watchman continued his discourse with the ease and eloquence of a man learned in the true history of the earth and its peoples. He was blessed with visionary perception and a cogent and clear delivery that made even the most arcane concepts accessible. His understanding of the inner mysteries of consciousness demonstrated a profound knowing, deeply connected with the collective knowledge of humankind. How he came to be the bearer of this legacy was a mystery in itself, and certainly one that begged further explanation. However, this night he would forge ahead with the determination of one who carried the burden of a sacred mission, and who would not be dissuaded from his appointed task. And so, as the evening stars created a backdrop to the wind-swept plateau of pyramids, a teaching was revealed.

"The early Egyptian religious and spiritual writings contain the oldest known teachings on the relationship between God and man," spoke the Night Watchman as he settled into his place by the fire. "The greatest achievements of the ancient Egyptians were brought about through their understanding of human consciousness. Although much more is known about their monumental architecture, sculpture and funerary rites, it was their insight into the hidden reaches of the mind and soul of man that was their crowning achievement. The depth of their insight easily surpasses that of modern psychology and formed the basis of an enlightened awareness whose influence was felt far beyond their own borders and times. Much of the wisdom of the early Greek civilization was attributed to knowledge gleaned from the Egyptians, who were already immortalized in myth when the Greeks were just beginning.

"The Osirian mystery schools taught that a human being was more than a physical form contacting the world through the senses. They recognized that the human form was the vehicle of expression for a complex of interdependent spirits they called the *ka, ba* and *Aakhu*. In many ways, this insight was re-discovered by modern psychologists who identified the existence of the sub-conscious, the conscious and the super-consciousness. Freudian psychologists called these aspects of the personality the id, ego and super-ego, considering them to be unintegrated parts of the whole being. The ancient Egyptians regarded these centers of awareness as separate but cooperative spirits. In this way, they were able to explain the seemingly dissociated nature of the personality, particularly where emotion, memory, thought, and conscience were concerned. It was their ability to define the nature of human consciousness and the forces through which it manifested in life that led them to master self-awareness."

"I understand the conscious, sub-conscious and super-conscious, as these concepts have been clearly defined by the science of psychology. Can you explain how they relate to these three spirits?" Raj asked.

"Yes, of course," the Night Watchman responded. "The spirit trinity–the ka, ba and Aakhu, are our immaterial, surviving essences. They transcend death, manifesting immortal, permanent existence. Because of this, they were of great interest to the ancient Egyptian priests who understood that to cultivate complete integration of these 'spirits' was to attain mastery in the three worlds (physical, emotional and mental). Harmony and perfected cooperation of these spirits within the core personality resulted in a fully-integrated, self-conscious, and divinely inspired human being. This was an enlightened being, one whose participation in the greater whole of society had an uplifting effect, aiding human evolution. But to give you deeper insight into this understanding, let me describe these spirits and their vehicles of manifestation."

The Night Watchman shifted in his chair, cleared his throat and

Of Ka, Ba and Aakhu

continued, "The foundation of Egyptian knowledge concerning the human constitution began with the physical body, which they called the *khat*. Because they did not attribute a spirit essence to it, they described the khat as a vehicle for the expression of the ka, ba and Aakhu. The khat is our physical form and, as such, is born, grows old, and dies. It is the khat whose heart beats in unconscious conformity with the pulse of life. It is the processor of raw materials and eats and digests in its role as a living biochemical factory, liberating energy from food. Eventually, in death, the khat will be consumed and returned to dust, because it exists to be animated by the spirits within who bring the spark of life. To withdraw the spirit-life from the khat as happens after death, would bring disintegration to the physical form when the body breaks down into its constituent cells. No spirit, no life.

"The ancients also recognized an energy field that surrounded the body forming a matrix for the physical form. In modern esoteric literature this is known as the 'etheric double'. They called this energy body the *khaibit* and understood the relationship between the physical form and its energetic blueprint. The khaibit has an electrical nature whose radiations can be observed, by the sensitive, as a faint glow of luminous colors: an aura or auric field, varying in hue and intensity in relation to one's vitality or state of being.

"The khaibit has another interesting property, as well. It can be directed to project a channel or stream of energy that can be sent out through space. Once established, such a channel is the means to send and receive energy and impressions. This is the basis of the phenomenon called telepathy, or the linking of consciousness.

"Have you ever thought of someone and immediately received a phone call from them saying that they were thinking of you? In this case, the khaibit was projected through time and space, connecting the consciousness of the individuals. The khaibit, like the khat, was not considered to be an individualized spirit, but only a vehicle to be utilized, subject to dissolution upon death."

"So," interjected Raj, "the body or khat, and the etheric or 'energy body' called the khaibit, can only carry the consciousness, but they are not the consciousness."

"Exactly. These bodies are essential to existence, but without the informing spirits they are unconscious, having no emotion, mind or spiritual presence. In conjunction with the ka, ba and Aakhu, they become animated and sentient. This unique cooperation forms the basis of the personality, beginning with the ka.

"The ka is the youngest spirit within the person, and it was recognized as the source of memory and emotion–the subconscious. Interacting closely with the appetites of the body such as hunger, comfort, pain and lust, the ka is the originator of desire and is responsible for survival. As the creator of emotion, the ka can react with fear, anger, and sadness, or love, joy and happiness. It also receives the impulses of the physical senses and reacts directly to pleasure and pain. The ka creates impressions from the senses and offers these impressions for interpretation and understanding. It records experiences and the emotional reactions to them, which are the basis of memories accumulated from birth. These memories are stored in the subconscious where they are accessible to the sentient spirit–the ba.

"The ba is the self-aware aspect of consciousness–the one who speaks. However, the ba relies upon the ka to deliver, from the storehouse of memory, images and experiences that comprise its present line of thought. Memories stored by the ka are called up in associated groups, like bunches of grapes on a vine.

"You may recall having experiences where you couldn't remember a name or recall a fact in the midst of a conversation. This happens when you draw a blank in regard something you know. Then, you pause, almost as if to address yourself, seeking the information. In that moment, the ba is contacting the ka. In most cases, this happens instantly but, in some cases, the ka may refuse or delay a response, waiting for recognition or the satisfaction of some basic need. If this happens, the ba must be patient with the ka's response, until cooperation prevails."

"That sometimes happens to me," Raj laughed. "It's like having someone's name on the tip of your tongue, and not being able to remember it. Where are these misplaced thoughts? Are they in the mind?"

The Night Watchman smiled knowingly, paused and replied, "The stream of thoughts that comprise the consciousness at any given moment is the mind. Although we presume to have within our mind vast archives of memories, they are not a part of the thoughts that occupy our attention. Where is this memory and how do we find it? Modern science cannot explain this. We must call up the memory image and integrate it into our awareness. This indicates a distinct separation of the thinking process from the place of active memory, suggesting that these aspects of consciousness are quite different. Mostly, one thought will lead to another, providing the foundation for complex perceptions, because the ka groups and stores memories by association. But images and memories must be reviewed and rationalized by the ba for them to have any real meaning or relevance to the whole being.

"The ka is also inclined to serve its higher co-spirits: the ba and Aakhu. It loves to serve and thrives in this service. The reward for this form of cooperation is mutual, in that the ka must learn and experience the logical interpretations that are the hallmark of the ba's awareness for its growth and development, and the ba benefits by quick and easy access to important subconscious information. The ka develops self-esteem in this action, and the ba also gains access to a critical source of energy."

"What energy is that? Raj inquired.

"You see, the ka produces the vital force called sekhem, which it creates normally in the course of living. It utilizes this vital force to fuel the body's metabolic functions, releasing its potency into the blood stream. Additionally, the ka can also create a surcharge of sekhem through a special action involving the breath. This makes the ka an essential aspect of the human equation and a necessary link to higher consciousness.

"The training and cultivation of the ka is critical to everyone wishing to evolve to the full potential of their being, because the ka has domain over the creation of sekhem. It's also responsible for generating the channel that transmits sekhem via the khaibit or shadow body substance."

"But, how can I know my ka?" Tamera asked.

"We come to know the ka through caring and self-kindness. The ka is like a pet that thrives on love and attention. As the youngest of the three 'souls', it rarely acts with full cooperation unless it is trained to do so. Being predominantly reactive, the ka is capable of acts of unrestrained emotion or child-like behavior. Often, the ka is known to run away with the person, an action that usually has dire consequences. Picture what would happen if you allowed yourself to act upon every impulse that arose from your desire nature, whether motivated by lust, greed, jealousy or the like, and you can see how easily the boundaries of decency can be transgressed. Most people, having evolved to a state of responsible cooperation within society, have trained their ka to behave with integrity coexisting peacefully with others. However, those with an unrestrained ka can act impulsively without consideration and are often involved in anti-social or criminal acts."

"If the ka is the emotional side of the personality and can act in an unrestrained manner, how is it brought under control?" Raj said, probing further into the teaching.

"This is accomplished by a conscious action of the ba, the middle-self. The ba is responsible for guiding the ka in its development. If the ba approaches the ka with love, asking for cooperation in the experience of being, the ka will respond in kind and be a cooperative participant in the life of the individual.

"The ba is the conscious-mind-self, the spirit that speaks, and with speech comes the faculties of reason and communication. The ba looks out to the world through human eyes and makes contact with the world through its perceptions. It creates identity, the 'I am', through which we come to know ourselves as separate self-aware beings.

"Ba senses the needs of the ka and draws upon the ka's accumulated memories to build personality, adding context and emotional texture to its thoughts. Because of this close relationship, the ba was considered to be the 'soul' of the ka, but really the relationship is more parental. Ba teaches the ways of rational thought and moderated behavior bringing the ka into alignment with its purposes, while promoting integration within the whole. Cooperation is necessary to the successful existence of them both.

"The ba was represented in the ancient Pyramid Text inscriptions (the oldest recorded religious writings known), as a bird with a human head. The bird body represented its spirit nature, and the human head its sentience. The ba was closely identified with the heart and was also called the heart-soul or *hati*.

"What was also recognized was the transcorporal nature of the ba. You see, the ba can exist outside of the body, as it does in dreams and in certain states of meditation, when it is free from the constraints of the physical form. These out-of-body states use a vehicle the ancient Egyptians called the *sahu*. The word sahu itself means 'to be free' and indicates the limitless aspect of its capabilities. In fact, the word Sahu closely resembles the Sanskrit word *sadhu*, which is ascribed to Indian ascetics who wander around freely.

"In the sacred Egyptian Book of the Dead we are told that the ba entered into the sahu: 'Thou has received thy sahu, thy foot shall have no limit set to it in heaven, thou shall not be driven back on earth'. In this way the ba uses the sahu to soar into other realms of consciousness. The sahu is called, in other occult sources, the astral body, and it serves as the medium for movement in the dream world. The sahu was not considered to be a spirit, but like the khat, was a vehicle for spirit and was subject to dissolution upon death."

Keeper of Secrets

Raj spoke up, "I think I've experienced my sahu in lucid dreams in which I'm aware that I'm dreaming. It almost seems like reality, in the dream, but it's not and I come to that realization upon awakening."

The Night Watchman nodded in affirmation, then continued, "The sahu, giving the ba form and energy in the dream world, can also be used for 'astral travel'. This is a technique to consciously enter out-of-body states of awareness through guided visualization, meditation or the use of certain sacred substances. The sahu is used to project the consciousness beyond the physical plane, unencumbered by the constraints of time and space. The ba slips into the sahu at the moment of emergence into the world of dreams, or purposefully in deep meditation. This moment of transition is especially magical, as the ba can straddle both worlds, and awareness can be maintained on either side of the veil separating these states of awareness. The dream experiences encountered by the sahu are mostly ephemeral in nature, with the free flow of images brought up from the memory stores of the ka. These images are synthesized and unleashed as a barrage of circumstances woven into exotic landscapes which are the basis for many strange encounters. Sometimes the ba's awareness prevails and vignettes of the dream experience are retained in the consciousness as the ba makes the transition from the dream to the waking state. In this case, messages 'brought through' are known to be of special importance and can be examined for hidden meanings relevant to the individual's life. These messages might also contain oracles, or visions of prophecy, revealing information about the future."

"So the sahu is just as important to consciousness as the body," Raj observed.

"Yes. The importance of the sahu was never underestimated because of the impact that a lucid dream or out-of-body experience might have on the understanding of events in the waking state. We spend a third of our lives sleeping, and during dream experiences much of our psychological processing occurs.

Of Ka, Ba and Aakhu

"It is also known that sahus can meet in the astral world, interacting and sharing the same or similar experiences. For initiates in the sacred spiritual orders, techniques were given to guide sahus to exalted places in the astral realms where special classes were taught by great Masters. There they would be given instructions on how to accelerate their spiritual development. It was known that the 'Great Ones' could visit a worthy aspirant in the dream state and a give direct experience of their grace–called *darshan* by the Hindus. The sahu could also indulge in acts of lust, attracting the low spirits of the dream world, the notorious *'succubi'*, resulting in actions that might even manifest in the body as physiological responses to the astral stimuli.

"Because of its freedom of movement and the unlimited possibilities for experience, training the sahu was a essential component of the lessons taught in the mystery schools. But mastery of this realm was considered only an intermediate stage of awareness, a phase between the physical and the most noble state of being–that of the Aakhu.

"The Aakhu is the true spirit, the indestructible, incorruptible, imperishable, immortal and divine High Self. It is the inner guide or personal angel–source of inspiration and wisdom. The Aakhu is a spirit of pure light and was identified by the ancients with the stars and the heavens.

"The ancient Egyptians thought that when the Aakhu left a deceased pharaoh, it took its place in the heavens as a star–the ultimate being of light. They pictured their pharaoh taking his place among the stars to become a star in the body of Osiris, whom they called Sahu/Osiris. They understood the profound connection between the origins and the spirit.

"Utterly trustworthy, the Aakhu gently trains the ka and ba, teaching the ways of light by guiding its 'co-spirits' to the path of higher evolution. Expressing compassion, forgiveness and love, the Aakhu offers unconditional acceptance and endless patience. The Aakhu is known to be able to see into the future, having the capability of perception transcending reason, memory and time. It is capable of affecting the future as well, through a magical cooperation between the spirits. Through the Aakhu miracles can be performed including spontaneous healing, telepathy, the reordering of the future, and the invocation of divine grace. The Aakhu is the intermediary between the self and the divine. As such, one of the great secrets to invoking divine authority is to first integrate the Aakhu into conscious cooperation, for it is only through the High Self that more exalted spirits can be approached."

Raj inquired, "If the Aakhu is already evolved and realized, why doesn't it overshadow the ka and ba expressing its divine presence?"

The Night Watchman smiled at Raj's eagerness to learn, and calmly answered, "The Aakhu, in its infinite compassion, never interferes with the natural development of the ka or ba, allowing free will to prevail as a divine birthright. These younger spirits must be given the chance to develop at their own pace, to learn by trial and error. The lessons that lead to higher consciousness must be experienced, and the decisions necessary for spiritual progress must be made in full awareness and with complete responsibility. The Aakhu, of course, desires to assist and is happy to do so, but only when complete cooperation prevails. This will happen when the ba and ka reach maturity and their level of striving is genuine. When that moment is reached, the Aakhu only requests that the ba (in cooperation with the ka) invite the Aakhu into the life. Once invoked it will manifest as a cooperative and effective force within the person. Invocation of the Aakhu is the first step toward becoming fully integrated in body, mind, and spirit."

"What is the next step?" Raj wondered.

"Sekhem must be offered to the Aakhu in an act of loving sacrifice."

"Where does sekhem come from?" Tamera asked.

"It is through the ritual use of sa that sekhem is created, in an act of mystery and wonder. The sa is the breath and is considered to be the key to unlocking the secrets of consciousness and divine power."

"How does the breath do this?" Raj asked.

"Breath is the only action of the body that is both autonomic and can be manipulated by conscious effort of will. Ordinarily, breathing is an action that takes place whether we are aware of it or not, like the beating heart or circulating blood. Most of the functions of the body occur without conscious effort, because the khat is self-administering in the normal course of existence. Of course, we can deny the body food or sleep, but these actions will result in an eventual degradation of the life force, causing illness or death, especially if taken to extremes. In our everyday existence, the body receives food, water, and rest in order for it to perform its life-sustaining functions. This allows the consciousness to reside in a pleasant habitation while going about its business of existence. Within the body, each cell will regenerate, and each organ will perform its duty: cleansing the blood, digesting food, releasing energy into the blood stream, carrying energy to every cell, and taking away its waste products. Cells regenerate, the body repairs itself, and a symphony of biochemical reactions occur. These all take place without the least bit of effort on the part of the ba.

"Only the breath is given as a way to alter the physiological condition. By using the breath the ancients realized they could create sekhem–the divine life force. Sa is the key to creating sekhem and unlocking the portal of divine contact."

"But how is sekhem actually created?" interjected Raj.

The Night Watchman thoughtfully replied, "By breathing deeply in a deliberate rhythmic manner, an accelerated release of energy occurs within the blood. The ancient Egyptians recognized that within the breath is the essential element oxygen, which is brought into the lungs and released into the blood. There it is carried throughout the body in an action that replenishes and renews each cell. By breathing deeply in a series of timed intervals the body is filled with oxygen. When this is done (without the oxygen demand caused from physical exertion), a surcharge of sekhem is created. This charge can accumulate, creating an energetic capacitance in the khaibit energy body, available for projection, direction and application.

"Realizing that when one's breathing stopped their life ended, the ancients understood that the breath was essential to life. They also understood that the special properties of sekhem could only be created in the physical world, where matter can be transmuted into energy. They discovered that sa creates a sacred fire which activates the creation of sekhem. They also realized that through the accumulation of sekhem, a special power could be manifested which they sought to harness."

Raj spoke up, asking, "Were they able to transmit this technique?"

"Yes. The ancients developed and perfected the Sa ceremony where they ritually used the breath to generate sekhem. They did this by visualizing that with each breath a charge of sekhem was entering and filling their khaibit. Slowly, the neophytes practiced the Sa ceremony until they were able to generate sufficient sekhem to perform what we would call miracles."

Pondering this for a moment, Raj asked, "What were these miracles? And, how was sekhem used?"

The Night Watchman paused stroking his chin and answered, "When this technique was mastered it was used in healing, and remarkable cures were effected. When channeled through the hands it caused broken bones to mend spontaneously. This is the basis for the healing technique called the 'laying-on of hands'. Projecting this energy into the environment they were able to control the forces of weather, causing it to rain as they wished. They caused the winds to blow at will, subdued the waves and currents of the oceans, and thereby propelled their sailing vessels. They used it to control gravity and with it moved massive blocks of stone, manipulating both mass and weight. By this power they built their monuments. Using it with plants they created potent medicines and abundant food. They also understood that sekhem could be focused and channeled for a profound spiritual purpose."

Raj, excited by these thoughts, pushed further, "What was this spiritual purpose?"

The Night Watchman cleared his throat with a low rumbling cough and continued, "The ancients discovered a special relationship between the subconscious ka and the super-conscious Aakhu in the transmission of sekhem. In order to facilitate this relationship, a link needed to be established between them. This link is created at the initiation of the ba (in khaibit substance), and is extended by the ka (and only the ka) forming a sacred connection with the Aakhu. It is within this channel that sekhem is conveyed as a sacrificial offering."

"But if the Aakhu is the higher spirit, why would it need sekhem?" Raj asked.

"Let me explain," replied the Night Watchman. "The Aakhu, on its plane of being, has a use for sekhem, but sekhem can only be generated in the physical world. Because the Aakhu is entrusted with the sacred mission of redeeming or 'spiritualizing' matter and returning it to spirit (in alignment with the evolutionary spiral toward God that all creation is striving for), matter must become spiritualized. Sekhem is matter transmutting into spiritual energy. By eliciting the cooperation of the ka and ba to present sekhem in prayer, the Aakhu can fulfill its mission to spitiualize matter.

"And, most importantly, the Aakhu can also give back the special gift of transmuted life force as an expression of gratitude and appreciation for cooperation in this most sacred work. This gift was called M'nh–the great blessing, the mana from heaven, the grace from upon high."

"How does the Aakhu create m'nh?"

"M'nh is created from sekhem in an act of spiritual transmutation, like changing base metal into gold. The Aakhu's exalted presence transforms the sekhem by increasing its vibrational frequency. But in order for the Aakhu to create the sacred m'nh, an offering of sekhem must be made. Sekhem is offered in loving sacrifice to the Aakhu along with a call or invitation for participation in the spiritual life. It is sent within a channel of projected khaibit substance by visualizing a stream of life force rising up to the Aakhu, accompanied by the physical action of rhythmic breathing.

"To elicit the cooperation of the Aakhu, the sacrificial offering of life force must be made. This is a critical understanding, for its misinterpretation has caused much confusion and pain over the eons."

"How so?" Raj responded perplexed.

"The real problems in ancient societies began when sacrificial offerings to the gods were misinterpreted to mean blood sacrifice. Although it is true that blood contains sekhem (because blood hemoglobin carries oxygen to the cells of the body), it is unnecessary to make a living sacrifice of animals or, worse, of humans. In fact, what is required by the Aakhu, 'our living god', is the sacrifice of the life force offered in an act of love. This 'feeding' of the god, not with blood or flesh but with pure life force, is the great sacrifice and fulfills the divine plan to empower spirit. From this transmuted sekhem the ba and ka receive a return blessing which results in an outpouring of abundance, love and good fortune.

"Also, the ancients understood that sekhem could be delivered with a 'seed thought' or prayer, and that the prayer, if made with a pure heart, was always answered by the Aakhu. This is the secret to creating or changing the future. When the seed thought is offered as a vision of the future (desired by the ba), and is sent along with sekhem (in a sacrificial offering), the Aakhu's response is one of 'watering' the seed thought with the sacred m'nh. This causes the seed to swell and life to grow within the seed. When this seed germinates and begins to grow it becomes the new future-reality in the world of the ba and ka. With this knowledge the ancients were able to craft their future, creating an existence rich in love and prosperity.

"The ancients offered the life force to their Aakhu and, in doing so, invoked the reciprocal energy of divine grace. This is true call and response, the invocation and evocation that completes the circuit of cooperation and leads to the integration of the three spirits, ka, ba, and Aakhu. This is the path of higher awareness and of accelerated evolution, where the integrated spirit achieves co-creativity with God, the Omniscient Ra."

The Night Watchman became still and started to breathe in a steady rhythmic manner. He took four deep inhalations, pausing on the intake of the fourth breath, and then fully exhaled. He continued to repeat this cycle. Raj and Tamera watched carefully observing every nuance of this process.

Raj could sense a power building within the Night Watchman and could feel an energy emanating from him. It caused the hairs on the back of his neck to stand on end.

The Night Watchman raised his hand and, murmuring a cryptic incantation, directed his hand toward a stone situated between Raj and Tamera. With an effortless gesture of his wrist, the stone seemed to quiver and then proceeded to slowly rise off the ground until it hovered motionless about three feet above the ground.

Raj sat in amazement, his eyes fixed on the stone. The Night Watchman slowly lowered his hand and the stone descended back to the ground. Raj and Tamera were speechless. They sat stunned in a moment of epiphany, when suddenly another shooting star tore through the sky, its trail etching its luminescence into their memories.

Keeper of Secrets

Chapter 14

A Teaching Preserved

Both Raj and Tamera were astonished by the Night Watchman's performance. He clearly demonstrated the awesome power of his teachings. They looked at each other, speaking volumes in their gaze, words no longer needed. Tamera smiled at Raj as they turned to hear more of the story.

The Night Watchman continued: "An understanding of human spirituality was encoded by the ancient Egyptian priests into the language destined for safekeeping in the envisioned land. Their purpose was to preserve truth and guarantee the survival of the sacred wisdom. Extraordinary architects of encryption, the ancients were adept in conveying subtle meaning in the nuance of language. Each spoken word conveyed a different level of meaning, with profound concepts implicit in the roots of the words. The root words were the foundation of the language, both spiritual and mundane. As long as they continued to speak their tongue, the hidden truth would be preserved, an aural record transmitted by human memory into the future.

"The key to revealing the hidden truth lies just below the surface. To ensure the transmission of the ageless wisdom, the ancients empowered special 'Keepers of Secrets' to pass down the codex through the generations, calling them *Kahuna*.

"A closer look at the root words of the word Kahuna reveals *Huna*, the Hawaiian word for hidden knowledge, where hu is 'a bringing to the surface', and na is 'belonging to'. Kahu means a guardian, or a keeper, of huna–the secret.

"Even the name Hawai'i was chosen for the meaning revealed in its roots. The etymology of this word reflects the profound meaning conveyed in the transmission of the ancient wisdom from the Egyptian to the Hawaiian language. In the Hawaiian language the word *'ha'* means breath and life. In the Egyptian sacred language the breath was called the phonetically similar sa. The ha is used as a way to create the life force called *mana*, as sa created *sekhem*. *Wai* means water and was used as a symbol to represent mana in Hawaiian prayers because of its fluid nature. The root word hawai means to purify with water. *Waiha*, a word where the roots are used in reverse, means to give mana by breathing and to request through prayer. Hawai'i, as the underlying meaning reveals, is the place where mana is created and a place where breath creates mana. The word Hawai'i is a powerful key to understanding how the sacred vision of the ancients and their mission to preserve the ancient wisdom were woven together. It reveals the presence of the creative life force and the purity of their paradise, envisioned and found."

"Again, it seems, breath plays a critical role" Raj observed.

"Yes, it is through the breath that the Hawaiians consummate their prayers. It is through breath, the Ha, that they generate the sacred mana, the divine, miraculous, supernatural power–the sekhem of Egypt. In ritual prayer, the Hawaiians send mana to the *Aumakua*, the High Self spirit, which the Egyptians called the Aakhu. Just as the ancients had the Sa ceremony, the Hawaiians performed the Ha rite, generating sacred mana and offering it in prayer.

"The Hawaiian word Aumakua conveys the meaning and essence that is the Aakhu; even the sound of the words are similar. An *Akua* is a God in Hawaiian; au refers to being yours, and *makua* is a parent. *Aumakua* is your parental self, the High Self. The sacred word Aum, so revered by the Hindus, also finds expression here as Aumakua. Aum is considered the one eternal sound, the cosmic sylable of creation and again akua is a god, or in this case the personal God of creation. The properties of the Aakhu and Aumakua are the same; both are the super-conscious spirit, the guardian angel, protector and guide–source of divine inspiration, wisdom and grace. It is to the Aumakua that all prayers are addressed and to whom the gift of mana is sent. All appeals to the Divine Presence must pass through the High Self.

"The Egyptian ba became the *uhane* in Hawaiian, which translates as: one who speaks softly–the conscious middle-self. Uhane reveals in its root words 'u' which means a state of being; 'hane' meaning 'softly' and 'to give life'; ne is a murmuring and ha is also the breath. Together they are the self that speaks softly and breathes to live, an apt description of the middle-self.

"As for the ka, the subconscious, we find the Hawaiian word *unihipili*, whose outer meaning is 'the spirit present in the bones'. The 'u', again, suggests a state of being; 'nihi' means to be unobtrusive and 'pili' means to adhere to or to be close, clinging or sticking. The nature of the ka was certainly just below the surface of the person, as 'nihi' suggests. As to the sticky, clinging aspect of the root 'pili', it is suggestive of the shadow substance called aka.

"The Egyptians knew the aka body as the khaibit–the ethereal substance that conveyed sekhem or mana. Aka means shadow or likeness. Projecting the aka substance is essential in creating a link with the High Self. The Hawaiians visualized a projection of aka, which they called the aka chord. It resembled a chord or rope that connected to the High Self. The Hawaiian demi-god Maui is often depicted using the aka chord to rope the sun, symbolic of his relationship with spirit.

"The aka chord can, however, become blocked by feelings of guilt or other complexes born of wrong action or perceived sins. This blockage prevents mana from being successfully offered to the Aumakua. A *kala* or cleansing was used to unblock the aka channel, so that the gift of mana could be sent. Kala means to free, or to untie, where 'ka' is an incoming current and '*la*' is the light. To bring in light was the way to clear the aka chord, unblocking the channel to the Aumakua. The act of performing a kala came in the form of an expression of forgiveness for a hurt caused, or by addressing an offensive action with an apology or restitution. This was a necessary step in successful praying, because without an open aka channel the sacrifice of mana could not be made.

"The word *akaaka* conveys the sense of a clear, luminous, transparent substance. This is the nature of the material projected by the unihipili (ka) in the act of prayer. The aka energy can be sent, when visualized by the uhane, the Middle Self, as a braided chord extending from the heart to the Aumakua. Upon this chord mana is transmitted, and an offering or sacrifice can be made. Once the offering of mana is accepted by the Aumakua a reciprocal flow of the beneficent *Mana loa* is sent."

"What is Mana loa? Is it like mana?" Raj asked.

"Mana loa is the higher form of mana–the Great Mana. It is recognized as a return flow of divine energy and is often represented symbolically as a gentle mist from the heavens. This mist can be experienced in Hawai'i in the aftermath of rain, when a warm lingering moisture caresses and nourishes everything. Mana loa is a beneficent force, a blessing of God, sent by the Aumakua as a soothing balm to the cooperative spirits, uhane and unihipili, as an expression of protection and love.

"When the offering of mana is made to the Aumakua, a seed thought can also be sent. This seed thought is called 'ano 'ano and is used to convey one's hope or aspiration in prayer. Ano means sacred and reverent, a state of holiness. In 'ano 'ano, the sanctity of the seed was recognized, for it is in the seed that all life begins. It is the seed that, in nature, is the Holy of Holies. From the blessing of mana, the seed, or 'ano 'ano, swells and the miracle of life begins anew.

"*Aloha*, the familiar Hawaiian word expressing love, affection, compassion, mercy and kindness (all the sentiments that open the heart), reveals in its roots 'alo' meaning to share, and 'ha' the breath or 'to share breath'. Breath, again, is the most sacred of gifts. To share breath means to share the essence of life, which results in a harmonious linking of hearts.

"Ra, the solar deity of the Egyptians, is La to the Hawaiians.

THE TEACHING PRESERVED

They venerated the sun and recognized the potent life force issuing from its beneficent rays. *La'a* came to mean sacred or holy–from the sun.

"Linguistic similarities abound, as each language bears the evidence of a subtle commonalty. In many ways the essential tonal textures were preserved as each nuance of vibration communicated a special sound which could not be further modified without diluting its potency. 'Ua' and 'au', common prefixes in Egyptian, are often found in the Hawaiian language's vowel-intensive style. The Egyptian masters were able to encode meaning into a living language, one that has been growing and evolving to meet the needs of successive generations while acting as the vessel of a great spiritual teaching, carefully shepherded through the millennia.

"So, my friends, you can see how these two unique cultures, separated by thousands of years and thousands of miles, are really quite related. Deep in the spirit of their beliefs, hidden in the texture of their language, is a thread connecting their faiths, and a code of understanding that is the foundation of the path to enlightenment.

"I give these insights to you, my friends, that you may carry them into the world and share them with all beings everywhere."

As the revelations of eternal wisdom carried Raj and Tamera ever deeper into their profound spell, a pale nascent glow emerged on the eastern horizon. The night had passed all too swiftly, and soon the day would break, and with it the sights and sounds of the teeming multitudes that struggled to make another day's living in a land of endless days.

This had been a sacred night, one that would live forever in their memories. It had been a great initiation for them, when insight and revelation followed one after the other, each more profound than the last, each eliciting deep understanding. The unfoldment of the ancient history of humankind and its valiant struggle to preserve truth and wisdom, had been woven into a glorious story that revealed an underlying sacred teaching. Implicit in this teaching was the formula for understanding the High-Self, a gift beyond calculation and one that would set them on a profound spiritual path.

As the Night Watchman finished his inspired soliloquy, a subtle energy pervaded the plateau. The camp fire flared up mysteriously as through whipped by an unseen hand. Though quite exhausted by the long ordeal, Raj felt a new energy, beyond a second wind, almost as if he were supported by the hands of angels lifting him gently. Their wings of light gave buoyancy to his weighted, spent body. He was certain that the plateau was filled with a multitude of "other souls"–the Masters perhaps, the ancient M'htm who in their exalted place wait patiently, hopeful that the signs left millennia before will be found and understood.

What hope for the future, Raj thought, if this knowledge simply evaporated in the desert heat? Implicit in the teaching is a responsibility to carry on the work, conveying it so that the living knowledge continues fulfilling the mission of illuminating the path of all who strive to cooperate with the forces of light. Tamera also hoped to carry the teaching to her people and to those who would serve the Holy Mother.

Raj arose from his seat and grasped the hand of the Night Watchman outstretched before him. *"Salaam Alekum,"* he said, as he bowed in respect, gratitude and reverence. He placing his forehead upon the upper side of the Night Watchman's right hand. The Night Watchman responded in kind by laying his hand upon Raj's head, giving him his blessing in a language Raj had never heard before, perhaps the living pronunciation of the lost ancient Egyptian tongue. With awesome solemnity, the Night Watchman pronounced the formula *"Sa Sekhem Aakhu"*. Raj felt the holy spirit enter into him as a thrill of energy that he experienced from head to toe. It was so powerful that he shuddered in ecstatic rapture. It was a sense of pure grace that Raj understood as M'nh, the Hawaiian Mana Loa, the Hindu *bhav*, or spiritual emotion. It was

The Teaching Preserved

created from an opening of his heart, the portal to the soul, and was a sensation which gave him direct experience of the divine nature of being. This direct contact was the crowning experience of his journey and the true transmission of the teaching.

Once again, Raj excused himself, with Tamera concurring graciously. They both acknowledged the depth of understanding that had been conferred and promised to return again the next night to continue the work. Turning around briefly to bid a final farewell, his heart filled to overflowing, his eyes welled with tears, Raj noticed that the Night Watchman had already disappeared into the confines of his battered old shack. They left, walking down the dusty path toward Giza and the hotel.

Raj's feet barely touched the ground. He turned for one more look, but the Night Watchman's shack was already out of view. They were silent as they walked back to the hotel, each lost in worlds of thought. Tamera kissed Raj gently and said goodnight as she left him at the hotel entrance in the pale dawn haze.

Keeper of Secrets

Chapter 15

THE HAND OF FATE

At 11:00 a.m. the hotel room curtains radiated a dull ochre glow from the late morning sun. The air-conditioner kicked-in with a rousing 220V hum, awakening Raj from a short night's sleep. Getting up, he parted the curtains, raised the window and drew in a deep breath of dry desert air, pungent from the pall of burnt garbage and fresh lawn clippings. Remarkable in the late morning sun, the Cheops pyramid filled his field of vision from corner to corner; its peak bisecting the dissipating morning haze.

The first order of business was to call room service, where he coaxed the kitchen into delivering a pot of strong coffee. He took a hot shower and quickly got dressed, determined to get out before noon.

Raj checked at the front desk, looking for Tamera but she was nowhere to be found. He decided to take a cab into downtown Cairo and was dropped off at Tahrir Square, not far from the Cairo Museum. Weaving his way through several streets and alleys, he walked toward he *Suq*, the section of town that teemed with commerce.

He was soon engulfed by the crowd and surrounded by densely-packed, closet-sized shops offering hand-crafted products and exotic foods. Small cafes were jammed with turbaned men smoking their sheeshas, while incense wafted uninhibitedly from street vendors. All this created an intoxicating blend of sights and smells.

Raj was drawn to a small perfume shop called "The Secret Eye Bazaar" by a young boy with a story of exotic perfumes, "mixed special." The shop was dimly lit and draped in flowing red fabric from ceiling to floor. Oriental rugs carpeted the floor several layers deep, and spotlights hung behind panels of carved lattice.

Keeper of Secrets

Although he enjoyed being seduced by the ambiance and settled-in for the "big pitch," he hoped to simply purchase some jasmine oil for Tamera. It was a gift he planned to give to her later in the day.

From out of a back room stepped a man with a pencil-thin mustache wearing a light blue polyester leisure suit. He proceeded to introduce himself: "Welcome, welcome. I am the proprietor, Salaam Abdul Raheem Jamal Mohammed Al-Haq. Welcome to my humble establishment where we make the best-in-world perfumes, just for you, special price."

"Mr. Al-Haq, your boy tells me you have an excellent selection of perfumes. Perhaps I can sample them?"

"Please, call me Salaam. I am at your service," he said, in a thick broken English. "We are oldest maker of perfumes in Cairo. We can mix here to make any scent, just for you. You like something for special lady?"

Raj could feel the hard sell comming and decided to cut to the quick. "I am only interested in pure jasmine oil, just the essence of the plant. Do you have such a scent?"

"Oh yes, but please let me show you some perfumes designed to please the ladies."

Salaam quickly disappeared into the back room before Raj could say otherwise. Soon to emerge, as if on cue, was a short young woman wearing a black skin-tight blouse. Her hair was long, jet black, and fell in tight ringlets whose aggregate mass looked vaguely like the hairstyles found on ancient Babylonian relief carvings. She was carrying a tray of sweet tea and two plain glass cups.

The tea ceremony, Raj thought. This could take some time, but it was obviously the only way he was going to do business in Cairo. Next came the oriental background music. Now they had it all, set and setting. Salaam reappeared carrying a large case filled with small cobalt-blue bottles, each carefully labeled in Arabic script. Salaam uttered something to the woman who dutifully began to pour the tea.

The Hand of Fate

Raj sipped the sweet mint tea as Salaam began to unveil his collection. Each perfume had the same overbearing smell. The only response they caused in Raj was the gag reflex.

"Please Mr. Al-Haq, I am only interested in pure oils of jasmine. These other perfumes are not to my taste. Do you have any jasmine oil?"

"Yes, of course, of course. I go get."

Salaam ran into the back room, where voices could be heard in some kind of commotion. Returning, he presented a single, dark blue bottle, and expounded, "We are experts in art of jasmine. We collect the scent from our growers. Many thousand flowers are extracted to make bottle. I don't sell pure, but for you, since you are my friend, I make special price. First you smell."

Raj opened the bottle and dabbed some of the fragrant oil on a piece of cotton. He placed it close to his nose and, inhaling deeply, replied, "Ishtah Alaek! This is the real deal, fragrant but not overbearing. I like this."

"You know Ishtah Alaek! Ah, I like you. For you very special price, only 35 pounds."

"I'll give you 20."

"No please, understand, many flowers make special oil. This is rare jasmine, you cannot find anywhere in world. Give me 30 pounds."

"25 or I walk," said Raj, feigning to raise himself off the sofa cushion.

"O.K. O.K. Il Humd' Allah, because you are my friend, I take 25."

"Deal," affirmed Raj.

Salaam wrapped the bottle in a small torn piece of newspaper while exchanging pleasantries and extolling the joys of capitalism in mono-syllabic, self-congratulating accolades. Raj put the package in his vest pocket and left quickly, sneezing on the way out.

Raj reveled in the street life of Cairo, stopping often to drink deep in the local experience: examining the wares, sipping coffee and smoking the sheesha. Each shop had something unique to offer, and everyone wanted to do business. "Business, business, business, maybe, maybe, maybe," was the cry he heard wherever he went. He stopped in several antique shops, but the only things he found were the standard commercial pieces, "made new to look old." Still, he managed to locate a few "finds": several small statuettes which he carefully wrapped in newsprint and slipped into his day bag. He also found, in a back-street jewelry store, a small, golden Eye of Horus (the "healed eye" given to Horus by Isis as a replacement for the one Set poked out). It was considered to be the "seeing eye of Ra" and was presumed to have great magical power. Although small, the craftsmanship was very fine. He slipped it on the gold chain he wore and thought about the protection it might offer, like Dr. Strange's "Eye of Alamagordo" from the comics of his youth. He felt complete in his adventure and wandered about the Suq absorbing the local color.

He thought about the Night Watchman and the sacred teaching imparted to him. The legacy of ancient Egypt alive and well in Hawaii! Who would have guessed? He was excited by the prospect of another night at the pyramids at the feet of his new mentor. He wondered what other legends and knowledge might be told. The afternoon melted into evening and the evening faded into night as he finally made his way back to Giza.

With darkness descending, Raj decided to make his way directly to the pyramids to visit again with the Night Watchman. He thought about finding Tamera but knew she'd be busy at work, so he decided to go alone. Taking a taxi directly to the base of Cheops, he paid the driver his fare, plus a decent baksheesh, and proceeded to walk the path toward the Night Watchman's plateau. The night air was unusually still. He wondered why he wasn't hearing the usual evening's revelry.

He enjoyed the hike to the old shack and was looking forward to another night of profound revelations. He knew the route and casually walked the path focusing on the edifices that flanked the trail. He let his mind wander back to ancient times, imagining how the pyramid grounds might have been alive with the footsteps of temple keepers making their evening rounds.

He also assumed that at some point the large flood lamps would fire-up, bathing the pyramids in colored light; a scene repeated again and again for each fresh crop of tourists. But there was no activity tonight. Perhaps they skipped a night, he thought, enjoying the quiet and the subtle interplay of shadow and light that enveloped him in a cocoon of mystery.

As he crested the ridge, he was surprised to see that the Night Watchman's campfire was out. He wondered about the time. Maybe it was too early, he thought, but his watch indicated otherwise. The old mud-brick shack was completely dark as he approached and the door was padlocked. He called out to his friend, awkwardly realizing that he didn't know his proper name. He began shouting "Hello, anybody here?" over and over, but to no avail. The place was deserted.

He focused his flashlight on the building, immediately noticing a strange pattern of pock marks that trailed up its side, gouging deep splintered holes in the wooden door. He noticed the shattered remains of the old glass window pane as the beam of light glanced over the marks. He also observed what he thought was a distinct pattern: it looked like gunfire. Shocked, his heart started to pound as he realized that the building had recently been fired on by a weapon of some kind. He decided it was time to leave.

Without hesitation, he started running down the trail toward the amphitheater. It was dark and closed; no Son et Lumière tonight. He began to have grave concerns for his own safety, even as thoughts of the Night Watchman and what might have become of him raced through his mind.

As the trail opened up onto the amphitheater grounds he slowed his pace. In the distance he could see a squad of soldiers. Realizing it would be a bad idea to encounter them, he walked in the shadows to avoid detection.

His heart almost burst when, from behind a wall, hidden from view, a dark swarthy figure emerged. In a terse, audible whisper he heard, "Mr. Raj, Mr. Raj, come quickly, come quickly." It was Mohammed.

Raj was relieved to see him and hoped he might shed some light on what had happened. "Mohammed, you scared me half to death, but I'm glad it's you. What's going on here?"

"Oh Mr. Raj, it's terrible, it's terrible. They've come. There was shooting and everyone was running for their lives."

"Who has come? Mohammed, who?"

"It is them, the Jihad. Many of them, five, ten, I don't know how many. They were cursing and shooting."

"Why have they come? What are they here for?"

"They came to find the Night Watchman. They cursed him with a *fatwa*, a religious decree, and said that the name of the Prophet had been blasphemed. I don't know how they knew of this, but they said 'the one who had blasphemed the Prophet should die', and they were there to carry out this fatwa."

"What happened to our friend?"

"I don't know, but I think he got away. They came up the trail shooting and shot up the watchhouse."

"Yes, I was just up there and saw the evidence of their actions."

"They were screaming vile curses. They are ruthless and will only tolerate their own narrow views. They wanted to kill him, but he is a kind and just man. I hope he made it out. I don't know." Mohammed, now visibly upset, broke down in tears for his friend and the trauma of his ordeal. He was shaken and quivered with each sobbing breath.

"This is terrible." Raj said, clearly upset. "We can only pray for his safety and hope that divine protection has taken care of him. My friend, I will be leaving now. It's too dangerous for me to stay. Tell the Night Watchman that I will pray for him, and wish him Godspeed, Insh 'Allah. Tell him I will carry on the work and that the message will not die. Can you remember this?"

"Yes, Mr. Raj. I will tell him. I hope that I will see him again. He is in Allah's care, Insh 'Allah."

Raj was shaken by the experience. He didn't want to get between the military and the militant Jihad, but his concern for the Night Watchman compelled him to take action.

Of course, he realized that he would probably be of limited usefulness, especially since he didn't speak the language, but he was determined to do what he could. He needed help from someone, someone local–Tamera. He needed to find her fast; perhaps she could help.

The hotel was abuzz with the news of the attack. Luckily, the hotel was under government protection and a small army was dispatched to protect the guests. The last thing the Government of Egypt needed was more bad press. Reports of tourists being attacked and killed, especially in the south near Luxor, had frightened away many hard-currency spending visitors who would just as soon vacation at safer, less volatile destinations.

Armed guards stood sentry at the front entrance, and a phalanx of heavily fortified armored personnel carriers were lined up in the street. A curfew had been imposed, and all foreign guests were forbidden to leave the hotel. Security was tight and there was palpable feeling of tension. Every soldier seemed to have his finger glued to the trigger of his automatic weapon ready to use it with little provocation.

As Raj entered, he was questioned and asked for proof that he was a guest. He was approached with the same militaristic routine he'd seen at the airport: "Passport, passport, we must see your passport." After he suggested that he had simply gone for a walk, he produced his identification and was let through with a stern warning against leaving the hotel for the rest of the night.

The hotel lobby had become a command center for the military's activities. Raj was ushered into a dining room where many of the hotel's guests had assembled. Most seemed bewildered by the ordeal, having been, for the most part, aroused from their rooms to be "identified." Some people were dressed for sleep, while others were suited up and dressed for a high society social event. Women with sequined gowns and stiletto high heels casually chatted with men in pajamas.

An old, balding man with a broad white mustache, dressed in a black trimmed, red silk smoking jacket and an apricot-colored ascot, walked up to Raj. Adjusting his monocle, he said with a thick British accent, "I say, old chap, you just stepped in from outside. What the devil is going on?"

"Islamic Jihad," Raj replied, "just shot up an ancient site. Bullet holes in ancient stones, not a pretty sight."

"You don't say. Rather rude I should think," he retorted, sounding perplexed. He continued to sip from a large snifter of cognac and queried, "How the devil is one supposed to get any sleep around here with all this ruckus?"

"Well, just keep sucking down the cognac and you won't have any problem falling asleep," Raj replied, wanting to get away as quickly as possible. "Sorry, old chap. Excuse me," he said smiling, as he turned toward the exit. He knew that he had to find Tamera and made a bee-line for the front desk, assuming the air of authority that usually got him through check points in difficult situations. He found the manager and inquired politely about Tamera. To his relief, she was in the south wing of the hotel, working in a separate suite of offices reserved for the night staff.

Trying to look inconspicuous he casually wandered down the hall in the direction of the south wing. As soon as he was beyond the visual range of the soldiers, he picked up his pace, winding through a maze of interconnecting hallways where he soon found the offices. Without knocking, he entered quietly listening for signs of activity that would tell him where she might be. He could hear the faint sound of a typewriter pounding a clacking rhythm from down the hall. He breathlessly entered the room and was delighted to see Tamera hard at work banging out some sort of document. She looked up from the typewriter and called out in surprise. Rising from her seat, she turned and threw her arms around Raj, planting a passionate kiss on his lips.

"Raj, my dearest. I'm so glad to see you. I was so worried about you. Are you all right?"

"Yes, I'm fine. Then you heard about the shooting?"

"Yes, the hotel personnel have been informed, but we weren't told any details. What's going on?"

"Well, the Jihad is active again and out to create havoc. They paid a visit to our friend, the Night Watchman, with the intent to either kill him or scare the hell out of him. In any case they were looking to silence him."

"This is terrible! Is he all right?"

"I don't know, and I have no way of getting in touch with him. Perhaps your cousin Omar can help us find him."

"Yes, you are right. We must go to Omar's. He will know how to find him. But, we must be careful. It may be difficult to leave the hotel. A curfew has been established for all foreigners and check points have been set up. There are soldiers all over the place, and they don't seem particularly happy."

"There must be a back way out, some kind of service entrance or maintenance road that wouldn't be traveled by the hotel guests–a road less likely to be posted with soldiers. Tamera, you know your way around here."

"Well, I mostly enter through the front entrance. However, there are some old site plans that are kept in a room not far from here. Perhaps we could find them and they will show us a safe way out."

"Good, lead the way."

In a back room, down the hall from where Tamera was working, they found a small storage closet filled with site plans that were drawn up before the hotel was constructed. They rummaged through the rolled-up documents until they found a map that showed an overview of the roads that surrounded the hotel site. Before the hotel was built, there were donkey paths in the area that were used to reach the pyramids from surrounding neighborhoods. They noticed an area near one of the trails that seemed to have been planned as a tennis court. The original trail led out toward the back of the property and from there wound its way into Giza.

"I didn't know they were planning to build tennis courts here," she said, pointing to the map. "They probably abandoned this part of the plan before construction. But you see this maintenance shed to its right? This building I know. If we go behind it and follow along the southern perimeter we will eventually reach an old trail which we can follow back into Giza. We'll grab a cab from there." Tamera hurriedly returned the maps to the storage closet, and they ran out the door.

They left using basement service passages and side walkways, carefully avoiding the soldiers who were posted at every building entrance. Except for a brief instance when they slipped into the shadow of a hallway to avoid a passing patrol, they encountered no one and were not challenged as they made their way to the back of the hotel. They found the maintenance building and walked out behind it until they ran into a six foot chain-link fence covered by thorny hedges.

"This is not good," muttered Raj. They continued to walk the perimeter looking for a break in the fence, but to no avail. "Well, are you ready to climb?"

"I'll give it a try," responded Tamera, sounding a bit uncertain. "I haven't climbed a fence in years."

"It shouldn't be too hard. Here, I'll help you."

Tamera made her way up and over the fence, with Raj following quickly behind her. They laughed together on the other side, especially at the hole in Raj's pant leg, torn by the spiky fence top. They found a clearing and followed it to a path which trailed toward Giza. The moon, still bright in the night sky, made it easy to sight the old trail, just where the maps said it would be. They were soon out on Pyramid Road flagging down the first taxi to appear and continued to Cairo.

The cab left them off a few blocks from Omar's apartment building so they could spend a moment discussing their strategy before jumping into the fray. They knew there was grave danger to address.

Tamera listened intently to Raj. She adored his voice and his way of bringing stories to life. He held her close as they walked, and they glanced at each other often as they spoke, exchanging gazes filled with longing. The simple act of walking together with Tamera drawn close to him elicited a sense of passion in Raj. Each step seemed as if it were part of a dream, with the magic of their past weaving a mysterious aura into their present, transforming the mundane streets of Cairo into a land of exotic splendor. The street light, dancing through the trees, cast playful shadows which accompanied their walk like a procession of attendants fanning them with peacock feathers and tossing rose petals upon their path. The royal existence that had once been theirs was theirs again, as they walked in the ebony Cairo night with the sweet fragrance of honeysuckle infusing the evening air. They knew they were experiencing a special moment.

It was from this dreamy, love-intoxicated state that they were awakened by a rather disturbing sight about half-way down the street. Four men appeared to be coming out of Omar's building from his private entrance. They were grouped closely together and were crossing the sidewalk toward a double-parked car. Raj and Tamera picked up their pace to draw closer for a better look at the situation.

Their hearts began to pound as the sensation of fear took hold of them. They could see the terrified expression on Omar's face as he was being strong-armed toward the vehicle, with the barrel of a hand gun nuzzled at his neck. His eyes flashed a warning, though he said nothing, the fate of his life precariously balanced in the reaction of an armed assailant.

Keeper of Secrets

Yes, it was Omar, Raj thought, as if to convince his disbelief. He was being dragged from his home against his will. Tamera lurched forward. Raj reached out to stop her forward momentum but she slipped from his grasp. She screamed out to Omar with a desperate cry, calling to him in rapid fire Arabic. She got their attention.

"Tamera, go back!" Omar cried, before he was pushed hard toward the car. Despite these exertions, one of the terrorists raised his hand gun and screamed a warning of some kind, an incoherent statement whose meaning was unintelligible to Raj. Tamera took another step, boldly closing the gap between them, when the world began to move in slow motion. Each agonizing moment etched deeply into Raj's mind in a cascade of freeze-framed images.

The first shot whizzed past Raj's ear. He was surprised by its pitch as it split the air like a buzzing bee disappearing behind him.

The second shot grazed his right arm, tearing cloth but not breaking skin. He felt its velocity and its heat as he observed the recoil of the firearm in the hand of its perpetrator.

This is insane, he thought, his mind racing in a vain effort to produce a useful strategy or some remark that could stop the unfolding events. He was powerless and at the mercy of actions that were now beyond his control. It was a lack of control he detested, made worse by a mind-numbing paralysis born of fear and confusion.

The third shot rang out with a deafening report. He could almost see its trail as it exploded from the barrel of the gun. Tamera lunged backward falling into Raj's arms and they both tumbled to the ground.

"Tamera! My God, no!" exclaimed Raj, in total terror and disbelief. "Are you hit?"

"No, I'm OK. But what are we going to do? Omar! Omar!" she screamed. "They're taking him, do something!"

Omar was thrown into the back seat of a dark sedan whose doors slammed in unison as it peeled out down the street, leaving black smoke and burned rubber.

THE HAND OF FATE

"I'll get help somehow." Raj exclaimed. He called out for help, but the surrounding apartment windows were closed tightly. "Please help us," he yelled. "In the name of Allah, please somebody help!" he called out again, panicked and distraught.

"It's too late, they will not help," Tamera cried, "they are afraid for their lives. My dear cousin Omar is in Allah's care now."

Raj was in a state of shock, but he knew that he had to get in a survival mode, because being in the midst of a kidnapping on the streets of Cairo was not a good idea for a foreigner.

He looked at Tamera and she at him in a way that spoke all that needed to be said. They both knew he had to get out of Cairo as quickly as possible. His association with both Omar and the Night Watchman had surely come to the attention of the Jihad. The danger was critical. They made the plans that needed to be made and, in a tense lingering embrace, affirmed their love and said good-bye.

Keeper of Secrets

Chapter 16

Epilogue

Flight 51, a non-stop 747 from Cairo to London, was packed with the usual cast of characters: businessmen in dark suits, pressed white shirts and ties; mothers with crying children; old men in turbans with tied boxes of unknown content; and women in floor-length niqab, veiled to the world, all with their own appointed fate. Raj had a window seat and was glad to take in one more aerial view of the Great Pyramids as the jet banked hard and turned toward the Mediterranean. His departure had been untimely, but necessary. It was too "hot" in Cairo, with the Jihad trying to suppress the truth in any form, the military everywhere, and him in the middle.

The Night Watchman had vanished without a trace and, luckily for him, not a moment too soon. The bullets that raked his shack were meant to kill, a destiny he seemed to have avoided. As the beneficiary of his wisdom, Raj had concluded it was time to go. He didn't think being executed by zealots or spending time rotting in a Cairo jail, implicated in a politically-sensitive investigation, would further his cause.

He was glad to get out of Egypt, though leaving Tamera was the hardest thing he had ever done. He felt safe now that the plane was in the air and he was removed from the conflict and on his way to deliverance.

Reaching into his vest pocket for some throat lozenges, his hand grasped a small package carefully wrapped in newspaper. Unfolding the simple wrapping he found the glinting blue vial of jasmine essence–the gift he had bought for Tamera but never delivered. He slowly drew it out, running his fingers across the label, holding the bottle tightly in his right hand. He brought it close to his lips as he thought about her and carefully unscrewed the cap in a deliberate motion, pensively caressing the glass as if it were her smooth, warm skin. He breathed in long and slow, inhaling its sweet fragrance, his heart filled with emotion. The fragrance reminded him of her, of the sweet love he had discovered and left behind.

Perhaps he should have stayed with her to find Omar and the Night Watchman, he thought, but he feared the police and, besides, there was nothing he could do. It all happened so fast. He leaned close to the window, staring blankly as the events of the past few days flooded back into memory. He gratefully savored each moment spent with Tamera, unfolding the events in his mind in a surge of images and feelings. At 20,000 feet it all felt like a dream as the plane crossed over the thin green veil that separated the Sahara from the azure Mediterranean.

He thought about the Night Watchman and his teachings and of the responsibility that such a legacy bestowed. The real work was just beginning, he realized. Now it was up to him to explore these great truths, to follow the path of those ancient explorers whose mission it was to preserve the great Teaching. He recognized that a trail must have been left along the way, and he was determined to uncover it. He wanted to find out the truth for himself, first-hand, knowing that this would require mounting new expeditions to search the world for clues hidden deep within an obscured and fragmented historical record–a difficult task, but a task made easier by the package he carried.

Raj turned his thoughts to the treasure buried in the folds of his now-safe, checked-in bags. For, despite the commotion and the tragic events that led to his departure, he had managed to acquire Omar's extraordinary pharaonic funerary mask.

He traced, in his mind's eye, every contour and defining line of the precious inlaid stones perfectly crafted in thick Egyptian gold, in the likeness of a long-departed, ancient soul, a soul whose journey was frozen in time by a culture that deified the very act of

Epilogue

crossing over into death. He visualized the weight of its mass by the sense of gravity it exerted, remembering how he had carefully packed it away, placing it in his bag close to other, minor archeological finds. He already envisioned the sequence of events that would walk him through customs, with an import license duly stapled into his passport.

He thought again about all that he had been through in a few short days, the lives he had touched and the transformations that had taken place–some exalted, some tragic. Although he realized the true treasure of his journey was the gift of knowledge linking the past, present and future and an insight into the human soul, he was comforted by the thought that his golden prize would fetch a handsome sum on the London antiquities market and would fuel his adventures into an unknown future.

Keeper of Secrets

Glossary

***Aakhu*-** (ancient Egyptian) the High-Self, superconscious, ensouling spirit of the three-fold nature of human spirituality. (see Aumakua)

***Adytum Sanctorius*-** (Latin) the holy of Holies, a ritual room used for initiation of neophytes into the spiritual orders.

***ahlan wa sahlan*-** (Arabic) hello.

***ahwah masbut*-** (Arabic) coffee with sugar.

***aka*-** (Hawaiian) shadow, clear, luminous, transparent substance, often found as a braded chord (the aka chord), ectoplasm. (see khaibit)

***Allah*-** (Arabic) God, a monotheistic supreme being revered by the followers of Islam.

***aloha*-** (Hawaiian) love, affection, compassion, mercy, kindness, a friendly salutation, both hello and good-bye, a term of endearment, to share breath.

***ano*-** (Hawaiian) awe, reverence, sacredness, holiness.

***ano ano*-** (Hawaiian) a seed, a seed thought used in prayer.

***antediluvian*-** referring to the time before the biblical flood.

***asp*-** a deadly venomous snake.

***Aumakua*-** (Hawaiian) personal god, the High-Self, superconscious, ensouling spirit of the three-fold nature of human spirituality. (see Aakhu)

KEEPER OF SECRETS

***Au Sept*-** (ancient Egyptian) an ancient name of the goddess Isis. (see Isis)

***Awakened Ones*-** enlightened beings who guide the evolution of mankind. (see Brotherhood of Ra)

***ba*-** (ancient Egyptian) element of the soul corresponding to the conscious aspect being, pictured as a human-headed bird. (see uhane)

***baksheesh*-** (Arabic) the payment of a gratuity or bribe.

***Benben stone*-** pyramidion-shaped tip of a Fifth Dynasty obelisk placed at a solar temple.

***bhav*-** (Hindu) spiritual emotion, being.

***Book of the Dead*-** ancient Egyptian book of spells protecting the dead and describing the passage of the soul to the land of the dead. (see spells)

***Brotherhood of Ra*-** enlightened beings who guide the evolution of mankind. (see Awakened Ones)

***censer*-** incense burner used to hold burning aromatic herbs and resins.

***Chephren*-** the Fourth Dynasty Egyptian Pharaoh associated with the second pyramid of Giza, grandson of Khufu. (see Kaph-Re)

***Cheops*-** the Fourth Dynasty Egyptian Pharaoh associated with the first and largest pyramid of Giza. (see Khufu)

Glossary

darshan- (Hindu) holy sight, the direct experience of a saint.

Dumbek- Middle Eastern drum.

dynasty- historic period covering the reign of a family group.

EAO- Egyptian Antiquities Organization.

Eye of Alamagordo- amulet possessing special powers worn by Dr. Strange in the Marvel comic book series.

Eye of Ra- magical symbol, considered the seeing eye of God, the right eye, the sun and spiritual energy, the life force power of the spirit to animate matter, known as the third eye or ajna chakra in the Kundalini Yoga system.

Eye of Horus- magical symbol, the left eye, the moon, nature and understanding, the power to "see the way", attributed to the eye poked out by Set in a battle between light and darkness.

fatwa- (Arabic) an edict or Islamic religious decree condemning a blasphemous act.

fellucas- (Arabic) single-masted sailing vessel used for navigation on the Nile river.

gelabia- (Arabic) Arabic traditional men's clothing, consisting of a single cotton covering, ankle-length and open at the bottom.

Giza plateau- area near Cairo where the Great Pyramids were built.

glyphs- (see hieroglyphic)

Keeper of Secrets

ha - (Hawaiian) the breath, to breath upon, life.

habow - vernacular for hashish.

hamdul el lah - (Arabic) Thank God, by the grace of God. (see Il'humd'Allah)

hati - (ancient Egyptian) heart-soul, consciousness of the heart.

hekau - (ancient Egyptian) sacred words of power.

hieroglyphic - picture signs used to write the ancient Egyptian language.

Horus - ancient God, son of Isis and Osiris, name given to the inheritor of the throne of Egypt.

huna - (Hawaiian) hidden secret.

Il'humd'Allah - (Arabic) by the grace of God, thank God. (see hamdul el lah)

Imhotep - architect, scholar, designer of the Step Pyramid of Saqqara, enlightened leader during the time of the Fifth Dynasty Pharaoh Djoser.

Insh' Allah - (Arabic) God willing, if God wills it to be so.

ishtah alaek - (Arabic) the cream off the top of the milk, in modern vernacular anything considered to be the best of the best.

Isis - divine Holy Mother, most ancient of goddesses, mother of Horus, wife of Osiris. (see Au Sept)

GLOSSARY

jihad- (Arabic) holy war.

ka- (ancient Egyptian) element of the soul associated with emotion and memory, the subconsciousness, considered the youngest of the ensouling spirits of the human spiritual constitution. (see unihipili)

Ka'bah- a sacred stone housed in a rectangular building located at the main mosque in Mecca, Saudi, Arabia and considered to be the most sacred Islamic shrine.

kala- (Hawaiian) a cleansing, to forgive, to pardon, to free.

Kahuna- (Hawaiian) priest, wizard, keeper of the secrets of Hawaiian religion and mysticism.

Kaphre- the Egyptian Pharaoh associated with the second pyramid of Giza, son of Khufu. (see Chephren)

khaibit- (ancient Egyptian) the etheric body or bio-electrical matrix underlying the human form, source of aka or ectoplasm. (see aka)

khat- (ancient Egyptian) the material physical body.

Khem- (ancient Egyptian) the ancient name for the land of Egypt, Al-Khem.

Khufu- the Fourth Dynasty Egyptian Pharaoh associated with the first and largest pyramid of Giza. (see Cheops)

kohl- a black powder used as eyeliner.

kways- (Arabic) good (masculine).

Keeper of Secrets

kwayiesah- (Arabic) good (feminine).

La- (Hawaiian) Solar deity.

la'a- (Hawaiian) sacred or holy, consecrated, from the sun.

mafesh mushkilah- (Arabic) no problem.

mana- (Hawaiian) divine power, miraculous power, psychic energy created by the breath (ha or sa), prana in the Hindu yogic tradition. (see sekhem)

Mana loa- (Hawaiian) great mana, spiritual blessing, return flow of grace from the Aumakua or High-Self.

M'htm- great soul, derived from the Hindu word mahatma.

Mansions of Eternity- name given to the pyramids of Giza.

ma salama- (Arabic) goodbye, go in peace.

masboutah- (Arabic) happy, just right (feminine).

masbut- (Arabic) happy, just right (masculine).

mastabah- (Arabic) "bench" mud-brick structure used as funerary monument.

Mecca- sacred Islamic city in Saudi Arabia, considered the most holy site in Islam.

Menkaure- Fourth Dynasty pharaoh associated with the third pyramid of Giza. (see Mycerinus)

Glossary

m'nh- (see mana)

Mota- a preparation of psycho-active herbal plants and resins used for consciousness-expanding rituals.

Muezzin- (Arabic) Islamic priest who sings the Islamic prayers recited daily five times.

Mycerinus- Fourth Dynasty pharaoh associated with the third pyramid of Giza. (see Menkaure)

necropolis- (Greek) city of the dead, Egyptian cemeteries.

niqab- (Arabic) traditional women's dress covering the eyes, face or body.

Nubian- a black-skinned Egyptian coming from the southern part of Egypt once known as Nubia.

Old Kingdom- Egyptian historic period corresponding to from 2,650 to 2,134B.C.

oriental- traditional form of Middle Eastern music and style.

Orion- stellar constellation revered by ancient Egyptians, identified with Osiris, considered the source of pharaonic power.

Osirian Brotherhood- followers of the cult of Osiris.

Osiris- God of the dead, paramour of Isis, father of Horus.

Oud- a fretless six-string musical instrument similar to a lute.

***pharaon*-** modern vernacular for pharaoh.

***Plan*-** sacred plan for the unfoldment and evolution of humankind.

***pili*-** (Hawaiian) to cling to, stick, adhere, touch.

***pole-shift*-** a geophysical theory regarding periodic changes in the location of the north and south poles.

***psychometry*-** the ability to sense the history and origin of an object.

***pyramid*-** four-sided structure composed of triangular sides culminating in a single apex.

***Pyramids of Abusir*-** Fifth Dynasty pyramids located south of Giza, also called the crumbling pyramids.

***Pyramids of Giza*-** a series of pyramids built by the Fourth Dynasty pharaohs Cheops, Chephren and Menkaure.

***Ra*- Egyptian God**, "nameless one", infinite cosmic energy, cosmic consciousness, God of light, solar deity.

***Ram*- Hindu God**, an incarnation of the solar aspect of Vishnu, king of Ayodhya he re-established a golden age of justice and happiness. "Ram" is considered the causal word from which all language issued.

***sa*-** (ancient Egyptian) the breath. (see ha)

***sabah al-khair*-** (Arabic) good morning.

***sabah al-nur*-** (Arabic) good morning, response.

Glossary

salam alekum - (Arabic) a friendly greeting used for both hello and good-bye.

Salvia divinorum - sacred psycho-active plant.

sadhana - (Hindu) path of spiritual discipline.

sadhu - (Hindu) follower of spiritual discipline, a wandering ascetic.

sahu - (ancient Egyptian) the dream sheath, or astral vehicle of consciousness used during sleep.

sarcophagus - (Greek) "flesh eater", a stone coffin in which mummies were placed.

scarab - (ancient Egyptian) dung beetle which came to represent the regenerative powers of the rising sun.

sekhem - (ancient Egyptian) divine power, miraculous power, psychic energy created by the breath or sa. (see mana)

Sekhmet - ancient Egyptian lion-headed goddess.

Set - the god of evil, brother and murderer of Osiris.

sheesha - (Arabic) a water pipe used for smoking tobacco and hashish, also called a hookah.

Shemsu-Hor - "followers of Horus" pre-dynastic leaders of ancient Egypt.

shinai - dual-reed wooden horn musical instrument.

shukran - (Arabic) thank you.

KEEPER OF SECRETS

siddhis- (Hindu) special extraordinary powers, physical, mental or psychic.

Sirius- revered star in the Canis Major constellation, identified with the Goddess Isis, considered to be the origin place of the souls of humankind. (see Isis)

spells- magical incantations composed for a specific purpose.

sphinx- (ancient Egyptian) Statue of a reclining lion with a human head.

stela- inscribed stone slab.

stupa- (Hindu) religious shrine.

succubi- (Latin) dream spirits of sexual temptation.

Suq- (Arabic) bazaar area where shops are concentrated.

telekinesis- the ability to move objects by thought.

telepathy- the silent transmission of thought from a distance.

uhane- (Hawaiian) element of the soul corresponding to the conscious aspect of being, "the one who speaks." (see ba)

unihipili- (Hawaiian) element of the soul associated with emotion and memory, the subconsciousness, considered the youngest of the ensouling spirits of the human constitution, "spirit within the bones." (see ka)

Uraeus- (Greek) a snake motif worn on the crowns of

Glossary

Egyptian royalty, considered to represent the third eye or ajna chakra center. (see Eye of Ra)

Ushabtis- (ancient Egyptian) small statuettes placed with the deceased to accomplish the work of the dead in the afterlife.

Venerables- enlightened souls. (see Awakened Ones)

wadi- (Arabic) a dried-up river bed.

wai- (Hawaiian) water, also used to indicate mana. (see mana)

waiha- (Hawaiian) to give mana by breathing, to request in prayer.

Watchers- enlightened souls who have evolved beyond the need of incarnation who observe and assist the evolution of humankind.

Zep Tepi- (ancient Egyptian) the "first time" as delineated by ancient Egyptian legend.

Order Form

Fax and telephone orders: 415 459-0281
On-line orders: rajagni@pacbell.net / order@agnihuna.com
Postal orders: Agni Huna Publishing, PO Box 51,
San Anselmo, CA 94979-0051

Please send the following books:
I understand that I may return any books for a full refund–for any reason, no questions asked.

❏ **Keeper of Secrets** $14.95
❏ _____ $_____
❏ _____ $_____

Company Name:_____
Name:_____
Address:_____
City:_____ State:_____ ZIP:_____
Telephone:_____

Sales Tax:
Please add 7.75% for books shipped to California addresses.

Shipping:
$4.00 for the first book and add $2.00 for each additional book.

Payment:
❏ Check
❏ Credit card: ❏ Visa ❏ Mastercard ❏ Optima ❏ AMEX ❏ Discover
Card number:_____
Name on card:_____ Exp. date:_____